DISTANT STAR

The Reminiscent Exile: Book One

JOE

D1445462

DISTANT STAR

The Reminiscent Exile: Book One

JOE DUCIE

Cedar Sky
Publishing

Copyright © 2012 Joe Ducie

All rights reserved.

All rights reserved. No part of this book may be reproduced or transmitted in any form, or by any means, electronic or mechanical, including photocopying, recording or by any information storage and retrieval system, without prior permission in writing from the publisher. One chapter or ten percent of this book, whichever is greater, may be photocopied by any educational institution for its educational purposes.

All characters in this book are fictitious. Any references to real people or real locales are used fictitiously.

Cedar Sky Publishing was founded in Perth, Western Australia.

This book also available as an e-book for Kindle.

First printed in the United States of America, 2012.

Written by Joe Ducie: www.joeducie.net

Cover artwork by Vincent Chong: www.vincentchong-art.co.uk

ISBN-13: 978-0-9873294-1-7

For FINOLA

First. Last.
Always.

Dark and getting darker, sweet thing, but you are my light.

Here we are as penguins (I'm the fat one):

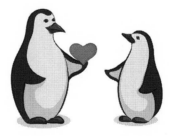

CONTENTS

SILENCE THE GUNS: PART III

ACKNOWLEDGMENTS

To the people who helped shape this story along the way — you are too many to name. But I'm going to try anyway, in no particular order.

To Irene Quinlan — my eternal thanks and friendship. You were right on every point, save for the wild berry cider. Strawberry & lime is far superior.

To Imogen Rice — you, your pens, and an awesome soundtrack.

To Andrew Ireland — Trail? Trail. You carry the Guinness.

To Scott Eadie — you're missing some good steak nights, bro.

To Chris and Val Ducie — for reading, for encouragement, for keeping the beer fridge well-stocked.

To Hamish and Rachel Cotton — for catching one or two corrections that almost made it into the final copy.

To Elisha Rooney — who taught me how to use a vacuum cleaner…

To David O'Boyle — you're not missing some good steak nights, bro.

To the bastards and bastardettes at DLP — no greater hive of scum and villainy.

Last but not least, to my editors at Red Adept, Becky Eaton and Lynn O'Dell — you humbled me good.

OPENING SALVO: PART I

Yet lost to time, that dusty trail.
A hangman's noose – a rusty nail!
The Never-Was King will command:
Degradation's demise at hand?

~The Historian of Future Prospect
After Madness, 2007

Regret for the things we did can be
tempered by time; it is regret for the
things we did not that is inconsolable.

~Sydney J. Harris

Islands of pure thought
Cannot compare Truth
Ah! Seen from aside
Naught but clouded cries.
Treasonous thought left behind.

~King Morrow's Lost Journal (Vol. VII)

CHAPTER ONE

Back in Black

"Why's it say '*ENTER AT YOUR OWN RISK*' on your door?"

I rang up the sale and placed the book in a brown paper bag. "Dangerous places, bookshops."

"No, really?"

"Really."

"What could be dangerous about a bookshop?"

The guy's smile didn't touch his eyes. Something wasn't right. I could taste strangeness on the air like burnt rubber, or smoldering pages. Two wars and a whole world of trouble while growing up had fine-tuned my survival instinct.

"Well," I said, reaching into my waistcoat. "There's a power in words, my friend."

His smile faded, and he made his move, tearing the brown paper bag apart to get at the book inside. He was sloppy and slow. I knew first-year Knights quicker on the draw than Smiler here. His ineptness was almost insulting.

I drew the novel from my inside pocket and slipped it open as the force of his Will slammed into me like a freight

1

train. Ah, such *strength!* I hadn't felt the like in years, not since the final days of the Tome Wars. He was young, too, his cheeks covered in a scraggly beard. I was nearly impressed.

Still, he did not know with whom he was dueling.

My book became an argent shield that obliterated the solid burst of Will, a pure power sent against me. I was the train and he, a Coke can. His fingers slipped across the pages, and he faltered, caught in an invisible net. Someone had taught him how to throwdown, but not how to focus his strength. Just enough to be dangerous. No matter.

His mind crumpled.

Blood ran down his face in rivulets from his eyes, and I snapped his limbs together, pinning him to the spot. He made a low, awful sound somewhere between a scream and a groan.

"Your name?" I asked.

The boy's Will had shattered. His copy of Figley's *Assassin* dropped to the floor, useless, just a book.

"Tell me, mate," I urged. "You must know who I am. What I can do."

I sent a wave of compulsion drawn within a thin network of suggestion and persuasion through the pages in my hand and across the boy's mind. Such subtle strands of Will were invisible to the naked eye, but they settled on his thoughts and dug the hook of my coercion in that much deeper.

"I am… the Pagemaster."

I snorted. "Really? We gave up those ridiculous codenames long before the war's end. Come now, tell me the name your mother gave you." The words on my book began to shine with a dark light. A *not*-light. Void light. "Or Lord Oblivion itself will be kinder than I will be."

The capillaries in his eyes had burst, staining the whites dark red. Through the crimson mess, I watched his small spark of defiance blur into fear, which was satisfying to see. I'd broken not only his Will but also his will.

"Je-Jeffrey," he said. "Jeffrey Brade."

"Jeffrey." I nodded. "A pleasure to meet you." I drew back a bit of my Will to give the kid a chance to explain. No one had been brazen enough to attack me for years. In a time not so long ago, I would have cast his soul beyond perdition without even blinking. "Why did you try to kill me today?"

He shook his head. "Can't tell you."

"Can't or won't?"

Jeffrey took a deep breath and released it slowly. "Won't."

"Listen to me carefully, Jeff. Can I call you Jeff? You made a choice today. You made a choice to enter my shop, to cast your Will against mine. I must say, you have one *helluva* talent. If I were anyone else, you would have had me." My tone hardened. "But I am not anyone else. I am Declan Hale, the Shadowless Arbiter. My Will is tempered steel, as dense as the heart of a distant star. Whoever sent you, Jeff, sent you to die. You owe them nothing."

"Fuck," Jeff whispered. "Fuck you. Atlantis is ours. You can't stop what's coming, Hale."

"So be it." The book in my hand was Roper Hartley's third adventure, a fine tale and as strong a cord as any in the Story Thread. The Dread Lord Astaroth casts Roper and the gang into the Blasted Pits of Na'ar—a place of eternal torment, of fire and lost souls. Call it Hell. "Goodbye, Jeff." The words leapt from the page, and dark light became a burning rope in the air.

Jeff's eyes bulged. "No, wait—"

Patience was not one of my virtues. The words wrapped around his neck like a demonic noose and yanked him forward off his feet. A tremendous burst of heat and energy obliterated his last scream. Like water sucked down a drain, Jeffrey Brade was absorbed into the words on the page. His form was scattered to the far reaches of darkest Forget.

I snapped the book closed and sighed. Five years had passed since I'd had need of that particular bit of power. Flecks of ash from another world swirled in the space so briefly occupied by Jeff, amidst the stink of burning stone and rotten eggs. Sulphur, fire, and smoke—I'd just sent a kid to Hell.

Holstering my novel, I stood for a long moment in contemplation before picking up the phone on the counter. I dialed the number from memory. The tone rang a single time, followed by a small click and then dull static.

"This is Declan Hale. A Renegade Forgetful just tried to punch me in the sack." What else was there to say? "Jeffrey Brade. Calling himself the Pagemaster. Obviously fancied himself some sort of wizard. He was trained in Will, but was sloppy." I paused. "Send only one, if you must."

A single exhalation of breath down the line preceded a dry click as the listener hung up.

~~*~*

I called Sophie and Marcus to make sure I was the only one who had been attacked and to summon them to the shop. They arrived a little before six o'clock with a third man in tow—a kid, in truth—who couldn't have been much older than Sophie. I'd put him at about twenty, given his wiry stubble.

"Who's this?" I cast my Will against the tall, lanky chap and sensed a wild talent in his heart. He was Infernal—Forgotten and Unfound—neither Knight nor Renegade, if I was any judge after all this time.

"This is Ethan," Sophie said, linking her hand in his. "I met him at uni. He has—"

"Some talent," Marcus grumbled. He stood brooding and impressive in the shadows against the True Crime shelves. His notable weight made the bulging cases groan. "And don't look at me like that, Hale. This is the first time I've met Sophie's apprentice."

"He's not my—"

"An apprentice can't have an apprentice," I said. "That's just silly. Ethan who?"

4

The boy cleared his throat and shoved his dark fringe back from his eyes. "Reilly. Ethan Reilly. It's an honor to meet you, Mr. Hale."

I smiled wryly at Reilly. "Sophie's told you all about me, has she?" The sweet thing had grace enough to blush. "Give me your hand, Ethan."

Ethan looked at Sophie, who nodded, and then he extended his hand toward me. I grasped it between both of mine.

"You should have brought him here sooner, 'Phie."

"We didn't think you'd approve."

"I don't, but here we are anyway…" I could sense Ethan's apprehension and anxiety. His Will was a thousand burning fireflies, blinking in and out of existence, swirling through his mind and soul. *Wild and wilder.* He had no professional instruction, which didn't mean he could be trusted, but it was a step towards that trust. "You have some talent, yes. A Will enough to navigate the Forget, even. But please tell me you haven't been doing that."

"The Forget?" Ethan snatched his hand back.

"Sophie not so forthcoming on that?" I laughed. "You're meddling with the power that burns at the heart of the universe, and you have no idea what you're doing. Sound about par for the course, Marc? Just swinging Roseblades in the dark, hmm."

Marcus grunted and took a sip from his hipflask.

"'Phie, you had to know this was foolish."

"Who I spend my time with outside of this dark and stuffy shop is no—"

I raised my hands for peace. "You're an adult now. Of course it's not my business. He, however, *is* my business. Untrained Will burns like a flare to others, like the Knights, or perhaps worse, the Renegades, who know what they're seeking. He has to learn to douse the flames. You *know* that, kid. If Tal taught you any—"

Sophie slammed her palm down on a mountain of leather-bound Austen's. "Don't you talk about her! *Don't you dare!*"

A tense silence clung to the heart of our little group, under the flickering light afforded to us by the dull chandeliers. For a moment there, in my arrogance—*always in your arrogance, Hale,* Jon Faraday whispered across time—I had forgotten Sophie's one rule. Never talk about her sister. Ever. I had no right even to her memory.

Ethan, for his part, put his arm around Sophie and pulled her close. She rested her head on his shoulder, fought back tears, and stared at me with more defiance than an army of Renegades. I loved her for that—for looking like her sister again. Loyalty to Tal had kept Sophie nearby since my exile. Just like Marcus, she had turned her back on the Knights and the Renegades—on Ascension City—for a shadowless traitor. I intended to see her loyalty rewarded one day, when I was no longer exiled.

"Well, I don't know what Sophie has told you, Ethan. But we're a merry band of misfits here. If you want to learn, we'll teach you. But it's not a game, that's for damn sure. Whatever Sophie's taught you, we'll probably have to start from scratch." I looked at Sophie. "I take it that's why you brought him?"

Sophie nodded. "Also because of the trouble you talked about on the phone. I know he has to learn to mask his Will, which we've been working on, but if there are Renegades in town... I'm not a fool, Declan."

"No, you're not. I apologize."

Somewhat mollified, Sophie shrugged out of Ethan's arms and sat on the front counter. She swung her legs back and forth. "So what happened today?"

"The past, I think, is about to catch up to me, though why now, after five quiet years, I've no idea." That was a lie. I had some idea. If anything, the Pagemaster's attack was long overdue. But some secrets had to be kept, even from this close circle.

And from Ethan, whose current status was New Guy: trust pending.

CHAPTER TWO

The Scotch is Callin' the Shots

"It begins, '*Tessa sat laughing by the rose bushes. A drop of starlight pooled in the cusp of the flower—*'"

"Hold on," Marcus said. He was drinking red wine from a champagne flute. Sophie and Ethan had left after a quick sip, in search of their preferred pre-mixed children's booze down the road at Paddy's Pub. Marcus and I were alone in the shop. "Rose bushes? Rose… bushes. I don't like that."

I pushed my reading glasses up the bridge of my nose. "The first line, and you already hate it?"

"You think with all these books you could find a better way of saying rose bushes. It sounds…" He waved his giant hand in slow circles. "Common. Too simple."

"You're being a touch persnickety."

"Persnickety? Really? Is that your word of the day?"

"Less is usually more when it comes to writing."

"Got anymore of the Merlot?"

I handed him the bottle. "The rose bush is important. The different colors of the roses lead to different worlds,

8

where Tessa can live in her memories. Red for passion, white for love, yellow for friendship... and so on."

"You should avoid the white, buddy. How long is this novel?"

I shrugged. "Half a million words, give or take."

"Less is more, huh? A Voidling would need a year to eat that thing."

"Shut up and drink your wine."

I saw Marcus out just before eight o'clock and wandered under an overcast sky into Riverwood Plaza for dinner. My shoes clicked softly against the cobblestones as I circled the large ornate fountain in the heart of the square. I studied the new addition to the cadre of businesses surrounding my shop in Perth's outer suburbs. An old man stood behind a small ice cream stand, set up out front of *Christo's Kebabs,* in the gunmetal light.

Thin letters scrawled in black paint were splashed across the side of a gently humming freezer trolley:

FROZEN BANANA - $2

"Warm enough night for it," I said to the proprietor. Three crystal vases adorned the top of his trolley, each containing a single, solitary flower: one red rose, one yellow daffodil, and one white lily.

The old man frowned and stared at me. His lips moved as if tasting my words. "You trade, boy?"

"Excuse me?"

"Banana for book." He pointed across the plaza at the dark and dreary storefront of my bookshop. "For book. With almond."

His grasp of English was poor, but his smile was honest. I shrugged. "Banana for book?"

He nodded, tapping a pair of tongs rather vigorously against the metal rim of his cart.

"Sure, I guess. Any particular requests? Chaucer, Tolstoy, Dickens? Which book, mate?"

"Which book... which book..." he muttered. "Storybook." His laughter boomed across the quiet courtyard. "Yar. A storybook."

Okay, a storybook. Or a book of stories. I nipped back into the shop and grabbed one of the ten thousand copies of *Grimm's Fairy Tales* I'd been hoarding for years. That book was like a bad penny—it never stopped turning up.

The old man handed me an icy banana dipped in caramel and coated in almonds. I gave him his tales and offered my hand.

"Declan."

"Mathias."

His grip was like iron, and his fingers were rough with calluses. You didn't get those from freezing fruit. Still, the banana treat was delicious, and I told him as much.

"Family recipe."

I nodded. My family, the few still alive, were scattered to and even beyond the four corners of all creation. Last I heard, my grandfather, the custodian of the largest library in existence, had been discredited because of my sins. Good for him.

"Why the flowers, Mathias?" I gestured to the three crystal vases resting on his trolley. The glass was pristine, flawless.

"Pretty, yes?"

"Of course."

"It would be forty years of marriage next month." He sighed. "I remember this... but I do not remember my wife's favorite color. These are nice, though. Pretty. I think she would have liked these."

Ah, damn. Well to remember that I did not have a monopoly on the infinite sadness.

We talked for a few more minutes. A buzzing streetlamp overhead cast Mathias's shadow against the redbrick wall behind him. It should have done the same for mine, but I'd long since forfeited my shadow... to gain lost and uncertain powers. I cast no shadow, not even on the brightest of days.

After returning to the shop, I locked the front door from the inside and flipped the sign over to '*Closed.*' An almost invisible ripple of power shimmered across the storefront, like a pebble cast on still waters. The night was quiet, which was always a touch unnerving. The wards, subtle enchantments of Will designed to protect from intrusion, were small comfort, but comfort they were.

I took a deep breath, embracing that familiar smell of good old hardbacks. Musky vanilla, shaved grass and a hint of wood fiber—best aromas in the world. The soft chandelier light cast flickering shadows over the books spilling off the shelves and stacked ten feet high.

"Rose garden," I said aloud across the empty shop. "Rose bush. Garden. Rose bed. Ah…"

The rough texture of the old books under my fingertips reminded me of afternoons spent in Granddaddy Hale's library. My store was a poor imitation of that immense catalogue. Through Biography and into Horror, beyond Horror to Sci-Fi/Fantasy, and then to the hallowed, white shores of General Fiction. *Here there be monsters.* The shelves ended in a small alcove with a window seat overlooking the street, where Marcus and I earlier had been sipping wine and critiquing terrible prose.

I slumped down with a heavy sigh and straightened up my pages. When I looked up, a man sat across from me chewing on a worn pipe. Smoke drifted in sparse rings toward the ceiling.

"Good evening," I said. "You know I can't help you anymore, old friend."

The English detective's brow furrowed and he leaned forward, placing a hand that felt all too real on my shoulder. "My good man—the game is afoot."

I closed my eyes, counted to ten, and thought of everything that shoulda, coulda, woulda been. Of Tal. When I opened them, the detective was gone.

But I could still smell the smoke from his pipe.

~~*~*

Some time near midnight, I awoke with a splitting headache and the dry, starchy taste of old scotch in the back of my throat. Whisky and wine—never a winning mix. I'd fallen asleep in the window bay, spilling a glass of red across the pages of my novel. Bothersome, but not as troubling as what woke me.

A silver orb of liquefied metal rippled in the space between the floor and the ceiling, pulsating gently. Short bolts of blue energy coursed along its surface, striking the dust from the piles of books and knocking a lidless bottle of scotch from the counter. A pool of amber liquid spread quickly across the floor. The orb was a construct of Will, of that I was sure, but not one I'd ever seen before.

A taste of copper clung to the air like blood on the tongue, or a mouthful of pennies. My wards were supposed to prevent this.

All the sound had been sucked from the shop. Standing up, I felt as if I were moving through tree sap, or trying to run underwater. The orb bulged, and a slit opened along its underside like a popped seam. A heavy, dark form wreathed in the silver light fell through the slit and landed with a thump against a stack of dollar paperbacks. It was a body.

And whoever it belonged to was laughing into the floorboards.

After all things said and done, I thought, for no reason, and could I smell... something that reminded me of Tal, of cherry blossoms in the winter.

"Declan!" Laughter again, but also a grimace. "Declan Hale, help me out here…"

The voice was eerily familiar. I stepped down and the strange arrival rolled over onto his back, perhaps sensing the same thing I did—that something was wrong. Terribly, terribly wrong.

"Don't keep me waiting, pretty boy."

He was ugly as sin, and I reacted with a harsh, startled breath. The man who had fallen out of the light, out of nowhere, lay in a widening pool of his own blood. Silver flames licked at his clothing, but they didn't burn. His eyes were *wild*. There was no other word for it. *Wild*.

He was also my twin. I was looking down at myself.

"Stop staring, sweetheart," Declan Hale said, and grinned one *helluva* bloody grin.

Drawn by the figure, I dropped to my knees. There was something clutched in his... in my hand. I reached for the object.

"Don't touch me—you'll create a paradox that'll destroy the universe."

I pulled back my arm. "Really?"

"No. Not really. But you touch yourself enough as it is." The man who looked just like me, save for an ugly, red-raw scar crossing his face, laughed. "I just wanted... wanted to tell you something." He frowned and motioned me close, using the hand that had been covering the hole in his belly. Blood flowed thick and fast from the wound.

I licked my lips. The world had slowed to a crawl. Sap hardened into amber, water into ice. "You're me?"

"And you will be me."

I stared at myself for a long moment, and then exhaled slowly. "How long before this happens?"

"You got just over a week. Grim forests in the dark, Dec."

I couldn't process that. "I can't save you from that wound. All the Will in the world couldn't... are you wearing my favorite grey waistcoat?"

"It looks better on me," Declan said. "And we both know I don't deserve saving. We're dead, Dec." His eyes were a little less wild. A little less... anything. He was not staring at me but through me. "Now listen. I am you. This is real. Call it time travel if it helps you sleep at night. It won't, trust me, but it'll keep you alive for... heh... for now."

"What are you—?"

"Shut up and listen." He was so pale. The pool of blood had spread under my knees. Broken quill! I was kneeling in my own blood without a scratch on me. "Train Ethan, love Clare, hug Sophie. *Forgive* the Historian. And trust Marcus, until he gives you a reason not to. And he will, oh my yes, he will."

"Marcus? He's earned my trust a thousand ti—"

"He's turned Renegade, but of the good sort..." His voice trailed away and his gaze grew beyond distant, beyond nothing. His breathing fell shallow. The rush of vital fluid had slowed to a trickle.

"No such thing, chief," I told him.

Declan lunged forward and snapped his hand around my neck, pulled himself up to shove his forehead against mine, and squished our noses together. A fierce, unholy heat was radiating from his ugly mug. I tried to look away and at anything but the living mirror. His grip was unbreakable.

"Don't be such an arrogant *fuck*," he growled. "And get a haircut. This ain't no painted desert serenade." He was mumbling, caught in that thousand-yard stare, a look I knew well. "Something else... something... Ah, yeah. Declan, remember, Tal *always* aimed for the heart."

He laughed again and fell away. The back of his head hit the floor with a sickening thud which made no difference. I was dead.

CHAPTER THREE

From Grace

Emily brought me a turkey sandwich around noon the next day.

I was sitting in my alcove, working on the novel and retyping the unsalvageable pages ruined by last night's accidents. I'd needed all of the early hours of the morning to dispose of and clean up after myself.

My body, I'd sent across the Void to the remains of Reach City, known these days as Nightmare's Reach, after the penultimate battle of the Tome Wars had seen the metropolis destroyed. I'd stayed tethered to this world and buried my corpse as I'd buried young Jeff Brade—along the ragged edge of the page.

Even so, the floorboards were stained with the blood of my... future good self? Of other me? The darkened spot would pass for a red wine spill.

"Good afternoon, Declan."

I looked up. "Emily, you make that dress look good." She wore a white summer dress with red straps that hugged her porcelain form. For the last few years, Emily had been my best and most loyal customer. More than that, at some stupid point we had become friends.

"Charmer. I thought you could try something a little different today. Turkey on toasted rye, with brie and cranberry sauce." She handed me the sandwich bag, her fingertips brushing mine. "What have you got for me?"

I ran my finger around a stain on the coffee table, a half-moon of dried port, unless I missed my guess. "The one you've been waiting for. Van Booy's latest."

Emily gasped and spun on the spot to face the mountainous stacks of books leaning against the loaded shelves, curving towers just waiting for a slight breeze. The gleam in her eye said *beware*. "Where?"

"Caught between Romance and Thriller. All wrapped up in a pretty red bow."

"Save me a bite of that sandwich." She disappeared into the endless maze of words.

The crumpled white pages before me were awash with red ink and even redder wine. I removed a comma from the third paragraph on page five hundred and twelve, then thought about it, and put it back in. Was there a difference between "lifted" and "raised"? An important one. Tal would have understood.

"She's a cute one, Declan," Roper Hartley, the magical protagonist from John Richardson's *Emerald City* series, said. "I've seen the way you look at each other. Don't you think it's time you got out of this dusty old shop and took a pretty girl on a date?"

I glanced up and then back down, shaking my head. Roper lounged on the leather sofa opposite me as if he had every right to be there, real and alive, and not some construct of Will or my own insanity pulled out of Richardson's works. "Pacing's a bit off in the middle here. Action, dialogue, action, and then exposition. Too wordy."

"I mean, when we fought Astaroth in the Vanished Empire you didn't balk at the idea of actual human companionship. What changed, Arbiter?"

I retrieved a fresh bottle of red from beneath the table. Add a splash of Jamaican rum and I was halfway to Sangria. Was it too early? It was wine o'clock somewhere. The alcohol would add some spice to the turkey and rye.

"The Emerald City needs you, Declan. Rumors of war in the Western Kingdoms have the goblin armies moving to claim Wildmen's territory. Evelyn is lost. If we can't find the Twilit Spear—"

"I'm a merchant now, Roper." I'd managed to ignore him for all of thirty seconds. He wasn't real. None of them were. They couldn't be, not in this world—the *real* world. "I sell books. I will not live them anymore. You'll have to fight the good fight on your own."

"Not everything lost is lost forever, my friend. You are too defiant for this."

There were a hundred books within two feet of me. A thousand more at arm's reach. In the store alone, I had over three hundred thousand unique stories. All those words and all those infernal *worlds*. Forever wasn't long enough.

"Please leave me be," I said.

"Hah! Found it!" Emily called across the shop from the region due south of Sci-Fi.

Roper disappeared sideways into a beam of sunlight with a carefree shrug.

"I heard you mumbling to yourself," she said, emerging from the stacks with her book in hand. "Stuck on a line?"

"Always. What's another word for 'affable'?"

"Friendly? Kind? Hmm… gracious?"

"I like gracious." A quick scribble corrected the offending word. "You're leaving again."

Emily nodded. "Hong Kong for a night and a day. How did you know?"

"You always wear the navy blue heels before you fly away and leave me."

"Do I?"

"Travel safe, Emily Grace."

~~*~*

Later that day I was paid a visit from my unofficial apprentice and her boy toy. They found me, as was standard, in the alcove sipping scotch and searching for poetic inspiration.

"Don't you two have class today?"

"Ethan wants to learn how to hide his Will from you." Sophie Levy bit her lip and glared at *her* unofficial apprentice, who was about to become mine, no doubt. "I can't sense his Will anymore, but I'm not as strong as you."

Truth be told, I'd sensed Ethan coming from three streets over. Masking the burning power was more art than science, more finesse than strength. Sophie's Will, her aura of supernatural strength, was hidden from me, even though my raw power outclassed hers by several orders of magnitude. Only a certain mindset could hide Will wholly and always.

"I don't want to attract anything nasty, boss," Ethan said. "Will you teach me?"

"Of course. We start as soon as you head across the plaza and fetch me a chicken kebab. Lettuce, onion, no tomato. Dash of hot sauce."

Sophie rolled her eyes as Ethan laughed. When he realized I wasn't joking, he saw himself out.

"He can be trusted, you know," Sophie said into the silence. We weren't often alone together. During our lessons, or whenever she had reason to visit, she usually made sure Marcus was about. "When I met him, he had no idea why he sometimes set things on fire with a stray thought. Forgotten and Unfound, as true as they come."

"We've been burned before, 'Phie. And by more than a stray thought."

Sophie nodded and said without any hint of malice, "Yes. And whose fault was that?"

After Ethan returned and I spent a good five minutes berating him for getting barbeque instead of hot sauce on my kebab, we got down to serious business. I closed up shop early and cleared some space at the front counter, knocking aside a few dozen sturdy books.

Messing with the dark, infernal powers of creation demanded pomp and circumstance, so I dropped a tea light candle on the counter.

"Light it, sunshine," I said to Ethan. Sophie looked on in mild amusement from the window alcove.

Ethan shrugged, whipped out his cigarette lighter, and ignited the candle's wick.

I grinned. Kid had a sense of humor. "Smartass. Do it with your Will."

"I've already got this down, Mr. Hale. Sophie taught me this basic stuff."

"I want to see you do it from the start so I can gauge how far to push you today. Can you light this candle? How about peel this apple with a thought? We always start simple. Now, light the apple and peel the candle." I closed my eyes and pressed my fingers against my lids. "And please, please don't call it magic. This isn't Hogwarts, and you're not a boy wizard."

"Okey dokey." He waved his hand, and the candle flickered to life while an invisible lashing of sharp force gouged narrow furrows in the apple's peel.

"How did you do that?" I asked.

"You know how. With magic-like powers."

"Don't be dense. Talk me through your process. How did you *make* it happen? Your Will is the tool, a doorway in your mind that opens on the fuel powering the heart of the damn universe. How do you, Ethan Reilly, step through that door?"

Ethan was shaking his head before I'd finished speaking. "No, it's not a door. Well, maybe it is for you." He ran a hand through his unruly hair. "I see... Well, I see..."

"What?"

"Promise you won't laugh?"

"No," Sophie and I said together.

Ethan raised his palms toward the ceiling. "You ever play *Super Mario Brothers*? The video game? When I do magic—sorry, not magic—whenever I use my Will, I see myself bouncing up and punching one of those question mark boxes full of coins." He snapped his fingers, and the candle flame turned a bright electric blue. "And it just works."

"Wow. Okay."

"Is that strange?"

I thought so, but then most everything was strange. "For no real formal education, you're doing just fine. At the Academy in Ascension City, we're taught from a very young age to think of stepping through a door into an ocean of raw Will. But whatever floats your boat."

"Water, usually."

"Ha. Ha." I summoned the blue flame from the candle and made it dance around my palm. The fire expanded, feeding on the air, until I held a sphere of coursing energy about the size of a tennis ball. The heat was impressive, but under my Will, the skin on my hands remained cool and unscathed.

Ethan watched, entranced. He was years from accomplishing anything this intricate. Despite my age—I was only twenty-four—fighting on the front lines of the Tome Wars had forced me to learn on a staggeringly steep curve.

"So how do I properly hide the Will? How do I... shut the door?"

"When people think of our power, they think it's a source to be tapped. But that's not how it is with our Will, not ever. If you have the talent, the ability to access it and use it to effect, as we do, then it is *always* switched on. All the time. There is never a moment you're not channeling the power through you, like the act of breathing—you're constantly doing it. You're lit up like a beacon for miles around, Reilly. We need to shut 'er down."

"How?"

"Up here." I tapped his forehead. "For me, I just make sure that the door in my mind is closed, which takes a bit of practice, but with the door closed…" The sphere of rippling blue energy in my palm spluttered and died. "You're about as Willful, or as useful, as a broken condom in a whorehouse."

Ethan snorted.

"Oh, charming," Sophie said.

"And what about Forget? Sophie tells me you use books to get across a void—"

I raised a hand for silence. "Not *a* void. The Void. A place, a level of existence that… sort of exists outside of the universe. I can't explain it better than that. Its very nature defies explanation. There are multiple universes. not just worlds, but universes. The Void is the space between them, a dark, ugly space… full of not so friendly things. Our Will can be used to traverse it."

"How?"

"Books—certain books—can be used to cross into Forget, from our world, this world, known as True Earth. You use your Will to invoke the words on the page. Again, certain pages, in certain books."

"The Infernal Works," Sophie said softly.

"Right." I picked up one of the paperbacks on the counter: one of Roper's earlier adventures. "Books that you can dive into, books that span the Void and cross over into Forget, are written by men and women who have some control, even unconsciously, over Will. Normal people, who can't use the power, have stories that don't become part of Forget. Their stories are just that… stories. You follow?"

"Not so much, no."

I nodded. "You'll get your head around the idea eventually, sure, and the best way to learn is to cross over the Void and actually travel to Forget. But we're not doing that."

Ethan slumped. "Why not?"

Sophie chuckled. "For one, the Knights Infernal will chop off Declan's head if he's caught diving into Forget."

"Oh."

I rubbed my neck, still firmly attached to my shoulders. "Yep, I'm in exile, Ethan. Times were, I'd have taken you to Ascension City and the Academy at the Fae Palace to be trained—trained properly. But I can never go back. Perhaps one day, when you've learnt enough to survive, you can seek it out yourself."

Ethan stared at me, frowned, and stuck his tongue between his teeth. He stayed that way for a long minute. "Can you still feel my Will?" he asked eventually.

"You're lit up like a forest fire, mate." I slapped him on the shoulder. "Fear not, practice makes perfect—every time."

"Can I ask…?" He glanced at Sophie. "Can I ask why you were exiled, Mr. Hale?"

"You can ask, sure."

Sophie rejoined us at the counter and jumped up onto her perch. As she swung her legs back and forth, her pink All Stars swished up and down Ethan's jeans. "Declan did some very good and some very bad things," she said. "There was a war in Forget. A hundred-year war that spanned time and space and universes. I've told you bits and pieces. Declan ended it, at great cost."

"That's a nice way of putting it." I poured myself two fingers of Glenlivet. I always had a bottle of it within arm's reach. "I pulled a kind of a dick move and crippled something called the Story Thread."

"The Story Thread?"

"All those other universes we were just talking about, written and accessed through the Infernal Works? They are part of the Story Thread, a cord of pure existence—of *all* existence—running through the Void and fighting the creeping nothing that is the space between universes. The Story Thread fills that nothing with *anything*, and has existed since the first Willful men and women put pen to page thousands of years ago."

"What happened?"

His question deserved another sip of liquid gold. "I unleashed the Degradation, which forced an end to the war. At the time it was a chance worth taking."

Sophie sniffed. "Never mind the unforeseen consequences, huh?"

"They were pretty damned unforeseen at the time, 'Phie. You think I wanted exile? You know what we lost—*who* we lost."

She relented with a sigh. "I know."

I turned back to Ethan. "Anyway, after the Degradation was unleashed, the Story Thread sort of... froze. I say crippled, because it can no longer support new universes, new worlds. I broke Forget. Every book written by a Willful author since the Degradation is *just* a book. Existing only on the page and impossible to use to travel across the Void."

Ethan played with the buttons on his shirt in the uncomfortable silence that followed.

I put him out of his misery. "There's a *helluva* lot to learn, kid. I'm pretty sure I don't have the time to teach you, which is why Sophie will take you to the Academy in a year or two, when you're ready."

"Is it like university?"

I laughed. "Oh good god, no. It's far crueler—like a military school for misguided youth. Since the war's end, perhaps the curriculum is more scholarly, but I doubt it. You're a lot older than those usually accepted. Twenty years ago, the Academy would've found you before your tenth birthday and shipped you off to Forget. The Tome Wars changed all that, and kids with the talent slipped through the nets."

"You started at the Academy at age *ten*?" Ethan asked incredulously.

"Actually, I started at six, but that's beside the point. You learn hard and you learn quick. Sophie spent three years there, eleven to fourteen."

"Do you graduate? Is there, like, a test, or something?"

"Or something. Students are tested constantly, in anything from enchantments to ward-casting, to augmented weaponry." I thought back to those days, almost fondly. "Then, at fifteen, you're sent on your first quest, called the Great Quest, which is a rite of passage for the newest Knights—a solo journey across Forget."

"Sounds... awesome."

"It is, in a way. You see, at that point in the training, the quest is more of a formality. The students have passed all their tests, learned how to command their Will, and traversed countless realms of Forget, under guidance. The Academy has been sending kids on the Great Quest for centuries, and really, its purpose is to allow fresh Knights to test their skills out in the real world."

"What is the Great Quest?"

"Nothing too special. Just find the road to the Lost City of Atlantis, and reclaim the troves of treasure and knowledge that vanished there over ten thousand years ago."

"Oh. Neat."

"Yeah, you see why the Great Quest is viewed as nothing more than a formality."

"Because Atlantis isn't real?"

I held up my thumb and forefinger about half an inch apart. "Close. After a thousand years of searching, no one has ever found even a trace of the city, beyond scraps of old parchment and half-whispered myths. My Great Quest was a bit different, however."

Ethan tilted his head. "Oh? You didn't have to go chasing after a fairytale?"

"No, no I did. Only difference was that I found it."

CHAPTER FOUR

Valentine's Day

I used to work for the Knights Infernal—an order of men and women dedicated to protecting the world from its own imagination. Terrible worlds existed inside books. Terrible, wonderful, amazing worlds of such depth and beauty, such tragedy and horror, that the ideas became manifest.

The fiction became a lie that told a truth, and a cord of the Story Thread.

The Renegades started off as a fractured cell of the Knights. They believed the Knights' power existed to unmake the world, or, more accurately, to reshape it, an idea that opposed everything represented by the Knights Infernal. The conflict between the Renegades and the Knights was one for the ages. They fought in shadows and darkness, in libraries and bookshops across the face of the True Earth and *in* and beyond the Infernal Works.

In deepest, darkest Forget.

They had all but destroyed one another five years ago, in the Tome Wars. I'd played a significant role during the war—I had ended it. My reward for forcing peace?

Exile.

Expelled from the Knights Infernal and barred from all of Forget.

I'd unleashed a horrific construct of Will that became known as the Degradation, and though the act saved many Knights and Renegades, I'd crippled the Story Thread to make it happen. Unbreakable laws had been broken. Lives had been lost. The one line in the sand that neither the Knights nor the Renegades would dare cross… I crossed.

The bell above the door chimed and I took a sip of wine. Two days had passed since the altercation with the Pagemaster, young Jeff. Light, purposeful footsteps clicked against the wooden floor. I heard the swish of a worn cloak. Clare Valentine stood before me in the window alcove. I'd been expecting her earlier.

"Hello, Commander."

"Just Declan now, Clare. You know that."

Clare offered me a sad smile. Her short spiky hair was a terrific shade of purple and green. She looked younger than I remembered, but then the last time I'd seen her, we'd been at war. Perhaps the five years since had been kind to her. I hoped so.

"Aye, I know that. You know why I'm here."

She didn't make it a question. The scent of her perfume, soft lavender, brought back a rush of pleasant and not so pleasant memories, of Tal and a sword of rose petals.

"Of course," I said.

In her right hand, Clare grasped a book firmly with her index finger between the pages, just as we'd been taught. She glanced around the shop, most likely for something more to say, her eyes roaming over the empty spirit and wine bottles littering the shelves and windowsill, before settling on the boxes of crinkled paper—my endless, imperfect manuscript.

"Now that," she said, "is perhaps the most dangerous thing I've ever seen. Declan Hale, storyteller."

"It is wonderful to see you, Clare. Were you sent to kill me?"

Clare smirked and offered me a sly wink. "Even five years away from the field, exiled beyond the Final Vanguards, you could still wipe the floor with me, I reckon."

I shrugged and stood, keeping my hands free and visible, and stepped across the space between us. She was a good two feet shorter than me, but her Will was one of the strongest in the world. "Faraday sent you."

"Yes."

"He very much wants me silenced."

"Yes."

"Hmm. He claimed the Dragon Throne unopposed, from what I hear." I heard very little, these days. "Probably for the best."

"Oh, yes."

"After Nightmare's Reach, after what I did?"

Clare paled and couldn't hold my gaze. "To speak of that is forbidden. Infernal Heresy, punishable by—"

"Exile? Death? All manner of unpleasant misery?"

Clare bit her lip. A strange thing happened. One of her green eyes turned as blue as a sapphire, and she laughed shakily. "Everyone knows what you did, but no one talks about it. They speak of... well, some say you should have claimed the Dragon Throne for yourself, Declan."

"That old thing? No, no. Faraday tied his own noose when he took that seat, and he did it with a smile. You wait and see."

"Jon Faraday is a lot of things, but he did keep the Knights together after the war. We owe him for that much." Clare reached out and ran a finger along the rim of my reading glasses. "He asked me to tell you not to interfere. We know the Renegades have licked their wounds, and small factions are regrouping. You should expect some reprisal, given your past. He told me to remind you that the only reason you kept your head was because of your service during the war. Declan, please, Faraday won't let you be a power unto yourself."

"It's not a question of who's going to let me, but more a question of who's going to stop me. My service is not the only reason I survived, Clare."

Clare's gaze turned wistful. "You always did love the classics."

I ran my fingers along the ropy scar tissue that stretched across her neck, from ear to ear. A madman had cut her throat, once upon a time, and she had died, ever so briefly. I leaned in close and kissed her cheek.

The book fell from her hands as she wrapped her shaking but strong arms around me. Her skin was soft, sweet, just as I remembered. Clare gasped, and the gulf of five long years between us may as well have been five minutes.

Her tears were salty and warm and she tasted like cinnamon and lavender, though our lips never met. To kiss properly was to make it real, and we'd never broken that rule and wouldn't break it now.

At least, I thought not. Clare gently brushed her lips against mine—a kiss, but only just, that changed everything. Oh dear, blood in the water.

I led her, and a bottle of merlot, upstairs.

CHAPTER FIVE

Jolly Folly

Clare dressed in a dusty shaft of sunlight. She took her time, too, rolled up her stockings slowly, one tiny foot poised on a stack of nineteenth century classics.

I admired the view from my bed. Late afternoon was bleeding toward dusk through the skylight. I had not felt this relaxed in years. Clare had always been good for my soul, ever since we were kids at the Infernal Academy in Ascension City. Two major war campaigns and twelve years stood between then and now.

Clare tossed me my pants, shirt and waistcoat. I shrugged into them with reluctance, not wanting our time together to come to a close. Maybe she'd stay awhile, if I asked. I joined her on the edge of the bed and slipped an arm around her petite waist. She had a familiar memory opened to chapter six.

"*Auron's Folly*," I said. A story about an evil queen and a prophecy that claimed her first child would both save and destroy the world. Some said it was a true story, as so many were, about the Renegades. "Still your favorite?"

Clare caressed the pages. "First time I've opened it in six years. Want to head inside?"

"Heh. There are two things I've not been inside of since my exile." I squeezed her close. "Well, one thing now."

"Oh, leave off."

"It's true. A condition of my expulsion was that Good King Faraday forbade me to dive in and out of stories. If I was caught, he swore he'd have me executed. You know that."

"Lord Oblivion itself couldn't keep you out of a good book. I don't believe for a minute you haven't been diving." She snuggled up against me. "I won't tell him if you won't."

"Ah, but what if this is an elaborate ruse, sweet Clare, to seduce me, lower my guard, and have my head chopped off and mounted above Faraday's gilded throne."

"You know me better than that."

"Do I? Then where have you been these past years? Jumping through hoops for the Knights? You should see them from my rather unique perspective." I shook my head. "Hard to tell where the Knights end and the Renegades begin, if viewed from outside the struggle. Especially given this tepid peace."

A flash of anger forced Clare's right eye from blue to crimson and back again. Only one fool could ever hope to provoke this woman and live. "You've changed," she said. "You've changed so much. Treason and blasphemy roll off your tongue like words onto the page. Broken quill! Declan, you were better than this."

And the truth of that was buried in fiction, wasn't it? Caught between one word and the next across the blasted wastelands of time. "I do miss the Drifting City, I suppose."

Clare placed her hand over mine on the pages of *Auron's Folly*. I felt her Will pressed against the book. According to the clock on the wall, it was seventeen minutes past five. The words upon the yellowed pages began to shimmer. The pressure in my ears was almost painful, and I again had that old taste of copper, like blood on the tongue or a mouthful of coins, as the dusty sunlight faded to black.

I added a drop of my own Will to Clare's invocation, and we slipped from one world into another, skimming along the dark impassable Void.

The sensation was always like walking into a cool mist on an autumn morning. I felt a rush of air as we crossed the boundary of nothing on the edge of everything. Then I caught a scent, like rain touching a hot road, as in my gut I had the sense of falling, falling so far and so fast that—

Clare slipped her hand into mine, and we stood upon a tall cliff face, looking down a vertical drop of over a mile at a vast ocean. Icebergs made of pure diamonds groaned along the surface. The stars overhead were alien, the constellations dimmed by the light of the twin moons rising to the east.

I took a breath of air so fresh and clear that I felt dizzy, or maybe that was from the height. Despite what the pretty woman at my side thought, I had not spent a single minute inside a book since my exile, and it was good to be back. Better than good, the feeling was like coming home. The countless realms of Forget were often more real than reality.

"This was always my favorite chapter," Clare said. "When the cities rise up between—"

"Oh, shush. It may not even come. Let's just watch."

We sat down together on the edge of the precipice and watched the moons swim across the sky. Minutes became hours, as the diamond icebergs bobbed along the dark water. After a time, lights appeared below the surface of the water—thousands of them. The night, the distant stars, were drowning.

Clare shivered and nestled in close. The air was silent at first, but then the grinding of gears and the tick-tick-tick of ancient machinery echoed up the cliff face. An entire city, a living, breathing metropolis, broke the surface of the ocean, ascending from the depths far below.

Miles across in diameter, the fabled Drifting City rose and fell on undulating waves, forcing large chunks of glowing iceberg diamond apart. Vast conduits and pillars sought hold on the base of the cliff. The shock vibrated up the mountain and Clare and I rolled away from the edge, lest we fall.

The city may have been in a story from our world, the True Earth, but here, we were still bound by the rules. Death here was still death. Many a Forgetful traveler had perished, mistaking reality for fantasy.

The living city sang as its struts dug deep into the mountain, seeking precious metals and rare natural resources for its growth. The mighty skyscrapers gleamed in the starlight. People rode the biomechanical beast, hundreds of thousands of them. The city was a wonder, an impossible, perfect wonder.

"I could watch that for days," Clare whispered. Both her eyes were the same color now, a brilliant burnished yellow. "I'm glad you came with me, Declan. This moment would never have been the same without you."

"Time to go, Clare."

Clare sighed yet nodded. Going back was easier than moving forward, so long as we remained tethered to the book back in my bedroom. We were tied to our real world, to the True Earth we knew best. If inter-dimensional travel could be described as *easy*, then it was simply imposing our Will against the magnificent creation around us. Letting go and falling back. The lights of the feeding city far below faded away.

I glanced at the clock on the wall in my bedroom. Coming up to nine o'clock back here in the real world. Hours had gone by as the city had drifted across the sea, shoving aside icebergs made of glittering diamond. Time flowed swift and true in both worlds, which meant I still had no explanation for watching myself die. If the Degradation had progressed far enough... but no, time was still wounding all heels.

Speaking of time. "I'm going to die, Clare. Soon."

"You sound so certain." She bit her lip. "There's something else I wanted to tell you, about a rumor circling Ascension City that Morpheus Renegade broke Aloysius Jade out of Starhold."

"Good for that homicidal son-of-a-bitch."

"Faraday couldn't prove it, but rumor is Jade was unchained in order to hunt you down and drag you back to Renegade's court."

Oh.

Shit.

All at once my impending death seemed far more… impending.

With the exception of myself, Jade had perhaps the highest body count in all Forget. He was a cruel bastard, too, but us war heroes often were. Jade had been my teacher, once upon a time, at the Infernal Academy.

"Heh. Five years of nothing and then this all comes to a head in just a few days. Isn't that always the way?" Fair but unfair. I shouldn't have survived the Tome Wars. "Silly to think I'd be left alone after the damage I caused. Silly to think I deserved to be left alone."

"You're frightening me now, Declan."

I nodded. "Aye, me too. Clare, we manipulate time when we dive into a book. Sometimes hours out here don't match hours in Forget."

"Yes."

"Have you ever heard of anyone diving into a book and emerging *earlier* than when they left? You know, technically travelling back in time."

"No. No I haven't. Surely that's not possible. It doesn't work like that."

"Apparently I did it—will do it."

"I'm not sure I follow."

Ah, well. "Lessons to be learned, sweet thing. Hey, did you hear I could've been a king?"

Clare shook her head. "I've got to be going. But I'll be back soon, I promise."

33

We lay in silence on my bed, wrapped in each other's arms for long, real minutes. "Take cake, okay?"

That was an old joke.

"Don't you mean take care?" she asked.

"That too."

"You just mind your books, Declan Hale. Mind them well."

CHAPTER SIX

Ships in the Night

So, the High Lord and King of the Knights Infernal, Jon Faraday, was up to something, of that I could be sure. No other reason to send Clare back to me. Besides pouring salt on an open wound, but even he wasn't that vindictive. No, there was more to the game that I failed to see.

I could consider his sending her as an act of kindness, if I didn't know the son-of-a-bitch so well. I had to add the Renegade attack and my untimely, still unexplained, future death to the equation... The game was afoot, but I was several steps behind the leader, which was unacceptable. Perhaps if I just avoided wearing my favorite grey waistcoat I could fight the future and live to see my twenty-fifth birthday.

"You have that air about you, Declan," Roper said. He scratched at the fierce scar that cut down his face and into the corner of his mouth. For a madman's illusion, he was remarkably well detailed. "You've met a woman."

"It was Clare, Rope. Clare came to see me."

Roper's grin disappeared. He was sitting only half visible, almost transparent, on my leather cushions in the dull light. "Ah, well. She was always a fiery one."

"You don't approve?"

I kept a steady beat on my typewriter, churning out fresh pages for the manuscript. One school of thought suggested getting it all done and dusted before editing, but there was no rhyme to that reason. None that I could see, anyway. Three or four thousand words a day was plenty.

"I just remember the last time you two were together," Roper said. "Entire worlds went spinning into the abyss. Lord Oblivion ate well that day."

"Sold my shadow to that guy, once upon a time." Atlantis was a wonderful nightmare. "You're thinking of Tal, who came after Clare, but thanks for bringing it up, either way."

"It is not something you should have forgotten, my friend."

My fingers slipped on the keys, turning *desert* into *desertyu*. "Do I look like I have forgotten the *Reach* for one minute?" My voice was closed, careful. I needed a tight rein on wild rage. "Bow-chicka-bow-wow, Rope. You're face to face with the man who sold the world. *You* best not forget that."

Roper scoffed. "Commander of the Forgetful Word. The Exiled King. The Never-Was Emperor… Shadowless Arbiter. The Renegades and Knights have given you so many names—and none of them even come close, do they? No, no." Roper stood up to leave, as much as an impossible construct of Forget-gone-mad, of Degradation, could leave. "Declan Hale, the man who ran. Hero turned fool. Conqueror turned coward."

I steepled my fingers beneath my chin. "Better a coward than a killer, good buddy."

"Aye, tell that to all who will die because of your inaction."

"I did act, Hartley. I acted when no one else would, or *dared*. You want a taste of the old times? My old self? Eight

36

million people lived in the Reach. They do not live there now… is that what you want?"

Roper tilted his head and appraised me in the dusty candlelight. "Huh," he said. "You've been using your gift, haven't you? What else could stoke the fires of your heart into such raw anger? Perhaps Clare is good for you, after all is said and done."

I would have responded with one helluva scathing reply, but at that moment the entire shop started shaking. Stacks of books tumbled onto the floor, and a quiet, subtle vibration ached through the wooden shelves. Together, Roper and I glanced up at the ceiling and the second floor.

"Is that what I think it is, Hale?"

I sighed and went back to tapping away at the typewriter. The words came easy, one after the other. Another shock rattled the glass in the windowpanes.

"Declan."

There was something fundamentally pleasing about using a typewriter, though finding ribbon for the darn thing was becoming difficult and expensive, too, but money wasn't an issue. Curls of dust settled on the table, shaken from the books and the tops of the cases. A low groan, almost below hearing, echoed from upstairs.

"Declan."

"I know, Rope." I removed my glasses and polished the lenses on my waistcoat. "I like to keep it waiting."

"Spitting in the eye of Oblivion, huh?"

"It's been five years since Atlantis and the Degradation. If he could do anything but piss and moan from the other side of the mirror he would have."

"How sure are you about that?"

"As sixpence."

Roper nodded, saluted me quickly, and disappeared. A snap of air filled the space he'd occupied. I ran my fingers along the dull keys of the typewriter and stood.

Upstairs, I paused before the bathroom door, my hand on the brass handle. Was the sound just in my head, or could

I hear laughter behind the door? Blood on the air, and that wasn't my imagination. I could taste the degraded Will on my tongue.

I let myself into the spare bathroom, a space I never used, and beheld the terrible mirror on the far wall, the Black Mirror, forged in a rusted cast-iron frame in the mountains just outside of Ascension City. The glass was tomb-dark and networks of deep cracks ran along the wall behind the mirror. The paint had peeled from the plaster and had gathered in small piles along the floorboards.

The mirror hung on nothing but air and only appeared to hang on the wall.

I had sold my shadow for this mirror, a lifetime ago.

I couldn't decide if I was brave or just stupid. I stepped across the room and gazed into the abyss. The glass rippled as if I'd cast a pebble on still waters. My reflection came into awful focus.

I raised my hand and so did the reflection. I looked pale, drawn. My brown hair hung in the cold sweat across my forehead, above dull blue eyes marred with black rings. I laughed.

My reflection didn't.

A dark, fetid oil spilled across the cracks in the wall. The substance was not-light, part of the ascending oils at the heart of the universe, the Will of the World, some might say. The oil ran along the cracks and bled down the wall. My reflection smiled and offered me a sly wink.

"Would you keep it down, please. I'm trying to write downstairs."

That wiped the smile from my face. My not-face made of not-light.

A hand came down on my shoulder and I turned to see all six and a half feet of the English detective staring down at me, chewing on his worn pipe. He regarded the mirror and the bleeding walls with a frown, a hint of disapproval creasing his face.

"Best you fix this, Hale," he said. "Best you fix this soon."

"I'd throw the darn thing into the fires of Mount Doom if I thought it would do any good, mate."

The old detective tilted his head as my dark reflection turned and walked away, back beneath the shadows of the Void, into the everlasting, forgotten sadness. A prime directive of chaos existed down there, of that I was sure.

"I fear your Will has weakened, my friend. I fear you are not what you once were." He shook his head and squeezed my shoulder. "Dark roads ahead, yes?"

"It seems likely."

Spirals of smoke drifted up toward the ceiling. "Then take this, Arbiter. You will have need of it."

He handed me his ear-flapped travelling cap, a tartan deerstalker.

"Excellent," I said.

"Elementary," said he.

CHAPTER SEVEN

Atlantis in the Sand

"So, latest news. I'm pregnant."

I dropped my red pen and took a quick step back. "Oh, oh wow."

"You don't have to stand aside. I'm not going to shatter, Declan."

Shatter... whispered Jon Faraday. The shop seemed to darken as the light was absorbed by some unseen chaos before it could breach the windows. I tried to keep my eyes from darting in rabid panic into the lengthened shadows and unknown corners of the shop—or worse, to the Black Mirror upstairs. I had a hunch it could sense my gaze.

"Declan, you're as pale as a ghost. Does the thought of a pregnant woman frighten you that much?"

The shop wasn't safe, had *never* been safe. "Emily... let's go down the road for a drink."

"You mean leave the shop? In two years I've never seen you set foot—"

Something fell a few stacks away, in the darkness, and hit the floor with a solid *thump*—a heavy hardback, unless I missed my guess. The characters in the Infernal Works only ever appeared to me, but did that make them any less real, here in the real world? I didn't know, and that scared me.

"—and in my delicate condition I can't be drinking alcohol."

"No?" I took Emily's hand and led her outside as fast as I dared, slamming the door behind us and rattling the square glass panes.

"Aren't you going to lock up?"

I could feel literary nightmares emerging from their worded prisons. The smell of dust and mildew. Two wars and five years of bad karma seemed to be catching up to me all at once.

"No," I said.

"But someone could rob you."

"If they can haul a quarter million books away before I get back they deserve to have them."

Emily's sandals clapped against the cobblestones as we walked down the road. A warm breeze wafted the taste and scent of fried hotdogs and kebabs from Christo's across the plaza. A weight lifted from my shoulders as the smell of old books dissipated.

"So," I said, letting out a long, slow breath I hadn't realized I was holding. "Who's the baby's daddy?"

Emily blushed. "I'm not... precisely sure."

"Oh? You sultry vixen, you."

"Well, it may have been Raphael in Provence, or possibly Damien in London."

"Wasn't there a chap in Singapore? Tall-with-great-hair guy?"

"Harry? I've not seen Harry in five or six months."

"Poor Harry."

Emily swatted my arm. We walked with our arms linked down Sugar Lane. The cobblestones were wet and glistening in the sun. I felt my books getting further and further away, and the distance was a knife to my heart.

"What a lovely day. I can't believe you're outside in sunlight, Declan."

"Have I tarnished my reclusive persona?"

"Quite tarnished, yes."

I snapped my fingers. "Blast." We fell into a companionable silence as we rounded the bend in the lane toward Paddy's. If I remembered correctly, the special on a Wednesday was the scotch fillet. "I should have guessed you were pregnant, Emily."

She raised a perfect auburn eyebrow. "Is that so? I've put on a little weight, sure, but not that much…"

"Heh. No. No. I didn't mean that." I gave her a quick kiss on the cheek. Emily was soft and warm and tasted like peaches. "Sweetheart, you're glowing."

She seemed quite satisfied with that. The day was nice. Sometimes, it was hard to remember the world outside the shop which was always there and very real, sure, but a thousand more just like this one were within arm's reach of my writing alcove. Still, perhaps I didn't want a scotch and steak.

"Let's walk down to the beach," Emily said, almost reading my mind.

I nodded.

The coast road was a five-minute walk down the street. Emily and I chatted about nothing, I felt nearly blissful. She was the only friend I had in the world that didn't belong, in some way, to Forget. She had no Will, no sordid past. I loved Emily for that. We crossed the road and headed into the dunes, along the winding sandy path that cut to the shoreline. The sound of waves crashing and the taste of salt on the air refreshed me, especially after a morning spent in the dark, dank smoky shop.

"You keep stroking your stomach," I said. "How far along are you?"

"Not long. Eight weeks, maybe."

"What do you think? Boy or girl?"

"Boy." Emily gave me a look of the utmost seriousness. "Most definitely a boy."

"So sure?"

"Women in my family always know, Declan."

I guess if I could dive in and out of fantasy worlds, and use my Will to violate the known laws of physics, then I could believe her certainty.

We kept to the hard sand just on the edge of the tide-line, a meter or so away from the swash. Emily's bright red toenails were encased in a pair of woven sandals which were more suited to walking in the sand than my black leather shoes. I undid the buttons on my waistcoat. The day was warm.

"Are you going to take some time off work?" I asked.

"Not for a few months, at the very least. We've got an important acquisition coming up soon. Lives on the line and all that nonsense."

"So you could be around more often after that? No more jet-setting off to exotic locations to meet with foreign gentlemen?"

Emily grinned. Her teeth were very white in the sun. "Declan, do you miss me when I'm gone?"

"Nope."

"You are a terrible liar."

A woman walking a golden Labrador offered a greeting as we rounded a curve following the surf. The day had taken a turn toward pleasant, and I didn't want to go back just yet. Lucky for me, the coastline ran for a good twenty-five thousand more kilometers before we'd be back to the start.

"You seem happier than usual, Declan."

"Oh?"

"Yes. One would think you may have had good news while I was away in Hong Kong."

Good news? Not so much, really. I was still no closer to figuring out how and when I was going to die, or what the Renegades and Faraday were up to. No one knew about the Mirror, save my merry band of illusions and Tal. None of them were going to be spilling secrets any time soon. The appearance of Clare was good news. Clare was *great* news.

"I saw an old friend. Someone I haven't seen in about five years."

"An old girlfriend?"

"Can you read my mind or something?"

Emily laughed. "Sweetheart, you're glowing."

A pod of dolphins breached the surface of the dark blue waters a quarter-mile offshore. Hand-in-hand, Emily and I watched them for a few minutes. I savored the silence.

"Look at this," Emily said. "There's a book half-buried in the sand. One of yours that got away?"

I knelt on my haunches and brushed some wet sand off a soggy and faded paperback. I pulled it out of the surf and turned it over in my hands, as if I'd uncovered some long lost buried treasure. In a way, I had. A poisoned chalice.

"*Tales of Atlantis*," Emily read over my shoulder.

It was on the list of books Thou Shalt Not Dive.

Hell, the book was the reason the list existed in the first place. The Knights did not make a habit of burning books. It was sacrilege—a heresy. But this book was one of the few exceptions that proved the rule, especially since the damage done because of the Degradation. What was it doing here? Right in my path? I looked up and out at the ocean, back around and along the beach up to the sand dunes. Was I being followed?

"Time to head back, I think."

"So soon?" Emily pouted. "I was enjoying seeing you in natural light."

"Would you have dinner with me tonight, Em?"

Her smile didn't ease the worry I felt about happening across a copy of *Tales of Atlantis*, but it didn't hurt either. "So long as you take me somewhere nice."

I tossed the book from one hand to the other and felt as though I were touching a live snake coated in pond scum—dangerous and altogether unpleasant. Only twice in my life before today had I ever held this book. The pages were soaked in enough blood to dye the Indian Ocean crimson.

"You, me and the scotch fillet special at Paddy's make three."

Emily rolled her eyes. "Declan Hale, heartbreaker."

CHAPTER EIGHT

Declan Dances

I let myself back into the shop after kissing Emily on the cheek and promising to meet her at Paddy's around seven.

I kept my wits about me as I moved through the stacks, mindful that I had left the shop unguarded for the best part of an hour. Anyone or any*thing* could be waiting to tear out my throat through my ass—

"And just what in hell were you thinking?" Marcus said, sitting in the window alcove with his arms resting on his knees. He looked furious.

"Pardon me?"

"You are *not* pardoned, Hale." The immense ex-Knight hauled himself up, knocked over his favorite champagne flute, and advanced toward me with clenched fists.

I held my ground. There were perhaps five people in the world that I would never raise a hand against. Marcus was two of them, despite what my dead self had alleged those few short nights ago.

"She was here, I know she was. I can *taste* her on the air, Declan. Like a battery on my tongue. She has a Will that is hard to forget, no?"

I often forgot that Marc and Clare had been more than Knights before my exile. "Oh, yes. Faraday sent her to investigate the Renegade attack. She—"

"You went diving. What in the seven hells were you thinking?"

It also paid well to remember that Marc was most sensitive to ripples of Will and cords of power use. When he said *taste*, he meant it. He could taste an invocation—smell the spell. *Helluva* talent. "I was thinking that I tire of this exile, Marc. That I hadn't seen Clare in five years, and she was like a breath of fresh air. Broken quill, she was *lovely*."

"You are out, Declan. The both of us are forgotten Forgetfuls—"

"We're gone but nowhere near forgotten."

He exhaled and relaxed his mighty fists. "You handed in your badge and your gun and walked away. To get mixed up in that again…"

"You wouldn't go back, if you could?"

He sat down with the slowness of an old man. "The Knights would never take me. I'm too stained by your shadow."

"Heh. What shadow?" I reached behind the counter and retrieved a bottle of Glenfiddich 15. "Come on now, let's have a sip and talk about what we're going to do. The Renegades will try again, and the Knights' renewed interest will mean trouble—for Sophie, and I suppose Ethan, as well—for which we're not quite ready."

Marcus took a long swig from the bottle. A drop of the amber liquid ran down his chin and blotted his collar. "Faraday will *never* rescind your exile. If you are even considering returning to Forget, to Ascension City, then you must overthrow him. But you do that at the cost of his peace with the Renegades. The one certainty in all this mess, the one unbreakable surety amidst the chaos and the maelstrom, is this: The Renegades would sooner see the world in ashes than you on the Dragon Throne."

He spoke the truth, but I'd be damned if the bastards thought they could get away with attacking me here.

"Let me say it again," said Marcus "You. Are. Out."

"I thought that for awhile, yeah. But now, Marc, now. It feels like... well... like the situation is how it was five years ago. War or something like it. I don't think I was ever out, not really—just benched. If anything, I'm deeper than I've ever been. Sing it true, pal."

Marcus threw up his hands. "Unbelievable. Just stay away. Don't go back. What's the worst that can happen? You have to fend off an attack once every five years?"

"Or, you know, I could end up dead on the floor of this shop inside a week." I shook my head. "But it's not just about going back, Marc... I walk down the street and see kids on their smartphones, sipping mocha-frappe-vodka energy drinks, or whatever the hell those things are, and I'm... I'm angry at all of them, at all the stupid ignorant people. They don't know what I've done for them—what Tal did for them. The only reason they're alive and not enslaved or worse is because of her sacrifice. They don't know. They can't know. I hate them."

"You are going to get someone killed. You know that."

"What's one more when my tally runs into the millions already?"

Marc had no answer.

~~*~*

Emily and I had dinner that night at Paddy's Pub, which was hustling, bustling, busy, and dizzy. Under the hot lights and cool air-conditioning vents, we sat at a table for two amidst the storms of laughter, song, and an altogether good time.

I had the steak, medium rare with pepper sauce. Emily chose the gnocchi, which I thought a rather brave offering for an Irish pub. The scotch was fine. Emily only allowed herself lemonade, given her condition, but that did not stop her from dancing.

After dinner, I watched her from a seat at the bar. She was the heart of the dance floor, and the live band, a group of old men singing ditties of the old country, kept in time with her. She moved with such grace, such subtle, timeless fervor, that every eye in the pub was drawn to her: a passionate queen in a little black dress, adorned with a silver crown of admiration.

After several songs, she remembered me, and sought me out at the bar. Emily giggled, her hair wild and eyes alight with the fire and the music—the noise. She sat down in my lap and kissed my stubbly cheek. "Dance with me, Declan Hale."

"No, ma'am."

She swatted my chest. "Are you going to sit there all night sipping that disgusting stuff while I get swept off my feet by all these handsome gentlemen?"

"Whoa. Hold on. Scotch is lovely." I took a healthy swig of liquid gold. "I don't dance. Never learned how, I'm afraid."

Emily laughed, the sound like water over pebbles, and kicked her heels into the air. If I didn't know better, I would have thought she was one glass shy of the bottle. "You can dance, but you don't want to."

"I'm telling you. Two left feet. I could shuffle and shrug my shoulders and that's about it."

"That's not the truth."

"On my life."

She stuck her tongue out at me and wrapped her arms around my shoulders. "No, never on your life. Declan, are you happy?"

I finished two fingers' worth of scotch between heartbeats. "I think so."

The music grew subtle and meandering. I imagined forest sprites flickering in the night. "Do you know what I think?" she asked.

"I think you're going to tell me whether—"

"I think you're so blinded by some past misery that you spend all day in that stuffy bookshop, drinking yourself stupid so you can write your novel and shut out the real world. You always look so sad, even when you're smiling. Especially when you're smiling." Emily ran her finger down the bridge of my nose and *tut-tutted*. "Let me ask again, in reverse. Are you sad, Declan?"

"I'm not drowning in happiness."

"What would make you happy?"

I didn't know. Who the hell did? Certainly not the face in the mirror. "Fish and chips a hundred years from now."

"What?" Emily sighed. "That's something else you do. You say the strangest things, and your words are always so careful and… and *proper*. I think you're trying very hard not to cry."

Visions of Tal being torn asunder, her soul and essence scattered into a machination of such brutal turmoil that even now the Story Thread still hadn't recovered, danced in my head. The Degradation. Our ultimate solution to the Renegade threat.

She was the girl I couldn't have.

"Shut up and dance with me, Emily Grace."

~~*~*

Emily walked me home that night, her bare feet silent against the cobblestones, her arm linked in mine and her weight leaning against me. I held her shoes in my free hand.

"You're a man, so you don't know how good it feels to take your heels off at the end of a long night of dancing. Whether through crunchy leaves or soft sand at the beach, walking barefoot is one of the best feelings in the world."

"You dance well. No one in that bar could take their eyes off you."

Emily smiled her secret smile. "You can't dance at all."

"Told you. I shuffled a bit."

"Oh, come on, now. You were—are—charming, Declan. And if you can be bothered to shave, you're even nice to look at. I think you abuse that—abuse the trust of the women in your life. Charm, good looks and eyes that look as if the world is about to end. What woman could resist?"

"Heh, plenty."

Back in Riverwood Plaza, we stopped for frozen bananas dipped in warm caramel and almond pieces. The vendor, Mathias, even gave me one of his dead wife's flowers for Emily, but I don't think he remembered why they were on his cart, and I didn't remind him.

A lily in hand, Emily and I sat on the rim of the fountain in the heart of the courtyard, my shop just dark windows across the way. Not one part of me was eager to get back to the scotch and typewriter. "Thank you for tonight, Emily. I forget sometimes, how simple it can be. Music, dancing…"

"You're welcome, Declan. I had fun. Anything that gets you away from all those books."

"I was just thinking that. But you don't like my books?"

"Too stuffy in the shop. I don't know how you breathe in there all day long."

"Well, I may be closed for a few days in the next week or so. Business trip."

Emily blinked. "Oh? Are you flying away? Off to see some exotic woman in some far-off land?"

"Something like that."

"I am both impressed and jealous. Here I was thinking I had you all to myself."

"Oh, you've never thought that." I laughed, and gently wiped a drop of caramel from Emily's lip with my thumb.

"So where are you going?"

"Some place far off and exotic."

"Really, now."

That night, after Emily hugged me goodnight in the doorway of my shop and drove home—as was proper—I lay awake in bed thinking deep thoughts. About life and love and all that was in between. Sing it true, songbird.

CHAPTER NINE

Nightmare's Reach

I didn't open the shop the next morning. Nor did I spend any of the short hours after dawn in front of my typewriter.

Instead, I sat with the remnants of a fine Pinot Noir in hand, and thought through my next move in a game that I still did not know how to play. I didn't even know against whom I was playing. Faraday, certainly, and perhaps the Renegade King. A copy of *Nightmare's Reach*—the same I had used to hide my body only four short days ago—sat unopened on the counter, next to the antiquated cash register.

True to my word, and my exile, I had only dived once since leaving the Knights and setting up shop in Western Australia, of all places. My dive had occurred two days ago, with Clare. Stashing my surprise corpse didn't count as proper diving, as I'd stayed tethered to this world and had just sent the body across the Void.

I needed to examine that body a little closer. I had questions that needed answers, which I wouldn't find if I sat around the shop in the dark. If I was to be believed, I had a little over four, maybe five, days before I found myself bleeding to death.

I took a long draw on the wine, tapped the rim of the bottle against my teeth, and decided to settle the matter. *Nightmare's Reach* felt about as light as a brick when I picked it up and flicked quickly through the pages. The passage I was after was on page one-hundred-forty seven:

…burnt orange light bled over the peaks of the snow-capped mountains to the west and a blanket of bruised purple sky shone with early stars to the east. Below that sky, Dremer sat in rumination of his fate. The ruins of Avalon smoldered with the heat of the Forsworn war machines. He remembered wondering if stone could burn. He didn't wonder anymore. The Reach was alight…

The passage was as good a place as any to dive into the story because it was close to where I'd hidden my body but far enough away to approach with some caution. I still had no idea what had killed me, or why, only that the violence happened at some point in my near-future. The concept was hard to wrap my head around, but caution seemed warranted, nonetheless.

Still, I hesitated just a moment longer. Marcus would come with me, if I asked him, and for that matter, so would Clare. No. I dismissed the idea of involving anyone else. For now. Afterwards, we would see.

I imposed my Will on the pages, and the words shone with Void light. The way between worlds shuddered and swallowed me whole. My shop disappeared with nary a whisper.

I stood in ankle-deep ash, right in the heart of Reach City. The air was cool, stagnant, and tense, as if waiting for something to happen. A book printed in Will afforded access to these lands of make-believe-made-real, but never into the story itself as it was written. Why would it? A story written down had already happened. We had the world after the tale, and this particular world I had ruined.

Once upon a time, I had given a speech here about victory and freedom—*sugar and spice and all things nice, boss*—and fighting the good fight. My words had gone on to bury about eight million people.

Here, the penultimate battle of the Tome Wars had been fought.

Here, I had killed a king and toppled an empire.

Here, Tal had conceived of the Degradation to seal away what we discovered in Atlantis. And from here we'd made the deadly race to the Lost City—madmen and demons chasing the two of us across Forget along the edge of the Void—and the end of the war. *Oh, Tal, how fast we ran.*

The Reach was a modern metropolis by True Earth standards. Before the best of my good intentions, the city had been vibrant and busy, but appeared desolate now from where I stood. Twisted and ruined husks of scorched cars lined the sidewalks, listing like broken fence posts under the weight of all the ash and rubble. Lifeless skyscrapers clawed at the dark clouds overhead, with piles of filth and bone swept into the doorways. Fire had ravaged most of the city, yet I could still make out small details, such as advertisements on the billboards.

Scattered all about the square were dusty books, remnants of the Tome Wars, spines broken and pages ragged. The stories were blank, spent, and small sparks of silver light danced about the broken worlds. A massacre in more than one sense had happened here, all those years ago.

No matter, after all said and done. I turned away.

Pools of starlight flooded the cusps of the tangled, thorny white roses growing where there should be no roses. The flowers had pushed up through the cracks in the warped roads, and thick, ropy green vines clung to the devastation. I thought them beautiful. Almost.

"You touch one Roseblade…" I muttered, and with a snarl ripped the nearest rose from the ground by its stem. The thorns pierced my palm and tore at my fingers. Drops of blood stained the petals crimson.

Clenching my fist around the blasted rose, I stepped lightly through the ash fall, each pace echoing down deserted city streets, and made my way across town to the safe house. The walk was long and lonely, through nothing remarkable. Everything was covered in grime and looked the same.

The small apartment was no different. In the story of *Nightmare's Reach* the place had been home to the protagonist's family who'd been stolen in the night by secret police for crimes against the corrupt state. In my story, the safe house had been a place to hide, to form unspeakable plans, and to fall in love, of all things, or the beginnings of love—of desire made real.

I'd hidden my body in one of the upstairs bedrooms.

The stairs creaked under my weight, and plumes of dust danced in small clouds around my feet.

"First one to fall in love loses. Ready, set..." I cupped Tal's cheek and kissed her lips. "Go."

Scratched into the paneled wall above the staircase was a bit of Tal's handiwork: our names enclosed within a crooked heart.

Silly girl. Silly, beautiful girl.

I didn't quite dare touch those splintered names. Call me a coward, but touching them didn't feel right after what had happened. We were nineteen. Young and in love. *That* old story. Carving the heart in the wall had been a hopelessly childish thing to do. But then, hadn't we been hopeless children? Hadn't we believed we could make a difference? End a war? Love each other forever?

"Two out of three ain't bad," I muttered.

Looking back, I knew we'd understood next to nothing about love, and when we first kissed and spent our night together, bleeding and bruised in this very room, lust, not love, drove us. Love came later, only a day later, when I watched her die.

In our special room upstairs, an old mattress sagged on a broken bed frame which hugged the wall. The shattered window looked out at ruin. Thick white rose bushes, again

55

where no rose bushes should be, grew up through the floorboards here, as well. Thorny vines and pure, untouched white petals brought back memories of Atlantis, of crystal swords, and of the end of the world.

Beneath all that, marring the dust and the wreckage, spread a crimson stain that could only be blood. The stain didn't look fresh, but then, it didn't look old. I guessed it had been created a few days ago, at most.

My body *had* been here, where I'd sent it, and the roses had grown after my body had gone. In between now and then someone had stolen my beautiful corpse.

Damn. The flowers were strange, but not entirely unexpected back here in the realms of Forget, given my sordid past and connection to certain lost powers. *Keep it simple, stupid.*

The roses were a sign from the past. Another sign, if another was needed after my death and Jeff Brade's attack. *Trouble, and in our road, boss.* At least the presence of the abundant bushes made my next move clear.

I would travel deeper into Forget.

Back to Ascension City.

But first I had to return to True Earth, to prepare.

CHAPTER TEN

Hunting the Transdimensional Whale

If I was honest with myself, and I'd long ago promised Tal that I would be, then I'd been looking for a reason to return to all I'd left behind, since my exile began. My death seemed as good a reason as any to go back.

The white roses alluded to a secret I'd left buried with a man in the market districts of Ascension City, and they were a thorn in my side that needed pulling. If this was to be my last battle, then so be it. I'd go out swinging and maybe take a king or god with me, before I was through.

Ethan was waiting outside of the shop when I stepped out of *Nightmare's Reach* in the late hours of the afternoon.

He was alone, which was odd. A small sliver of worry for Sophie made me flip over the ward enchantment sign and let him in.

"Glad I found you," he said. "I think something's been following me."

"Ethan, I don't really have time for—"

"No! I'm sorry, but you've got to listen. I can't find Sophie and she's not taking my calls."

I closed the door and flipped over the sign again. That tingle of subtle Will rushed through the shop. Ethan shivered, though I doubt he knew why. He was green. Despite my lessons, he probably still thought himself some sort of wizard or sorcerer.

"I'm sure she's fine, mate." I wasn't sure of any such thing, but I had my own hand to play, a lousy hand, really, without a happy ending. I wanted to say goodbye to Emily, but that wasn't in the cards, either.

"Can you... I don't know... 'Will' her a message, or something?"

"Will doesn't work like that. Ethan, perhaps you should start again. Someone following you?"

"*Something.* Something that moved so fast—and it was all dark, like a shadow. But a living shadow. With nothing attached to it."

Now he had my attention. "A shadow?"

"I could feel it at university, where I last saw Soph, and on my way over here," he said, "like an itch on the back of my neck." He scratched at his hairline. "I wouldn't be here if I didn't think it was real. I *saw it*, Hale!"

"I believe you. I do." I rubbed at my brow to ward off the inevitable headache. "Sounds like a Voidling."

Ethan paled so quickly I thought he might faint. He slumped against one of the stacks, knocking over a heap of Shakespeare and Austen. "I thought Marcus was just trying to scare me off. Why's it after me?"

I patted him on the shoulder and attempted a reassuring smile. "It just followed you to me, I'm sure. They took five years to get here, but here they are. It's probably skulking around the courtyard, zeroing in."

"You don't seem worried about that. It's going to eat our souls!"

"Thing is," I said, as if I hadn't heard him, "five years is nothing to these creatures. They exist outside of time. Outside of everything. From beyond the universe. All things

58

being even, it actually found me fairly quickly. I thought I'd be an old man before the Voidlings even bothered."

"So... bad luck?"

"Oh, always. But this feels like something else. For it to arrive now, of all times..." I gazed out through the fragile windowpanes into the brightly lit plaza, darting from nook to cranny and anywhere darkness could hide. With everything else that had happened in the last few days, the appearance of a shadow-ken could be no coincidence. "I think it had help. A guiding hand."

"Are we in trouble? Can I sneak out the back, or something?"

"Safest place for you is right here," I said and meant it. "Tell me, Ethan, have you ever used your Will to do damage? To hurt?"

"No."

"You're lying."

"I'm telling you, no!"

"Every kid plays with matches, mate, so give me the truth. I'm not asking if you've killed anyone, but shot a fireball into the ocean? Blasted a sphere of lightning at a Coke bottle?"

"Well, I guess I may have—"

"Good. Probably won't be enough, but good. This thing comes at you, hit it with all the coins bouncing around in that thick skull of yours. Go down swingin', chief."

Ethan clenched his fists and, for the first time, looked me in the eye. "You're insane, aren't you?"

"I think I'll go change into my black waistcoat." I'd watched myself die in the grey one. "Mind the shop until I come back?"

A Voidling was the broad and sweeping term for the collection of living shadows and other monstrosities that existed beyond the known realms. The Knights knew they existed. Every now and again, probably more often since the Degradation went so awry, they seeped in at select places in the world, holes in reality, and caused havoc. Voidlings were the antithesis of the written word, because they devoured not just flesh but aspects of the Story Thread itself.

For the most part, they were mindless. Those that crossed the Void into reality did so to *eat* and be destroyed. They were ridiculously hard to kill because, technically, they weren't alive, but they could be blasted to nothing with enough fire and ice and lightning.

But, as I said, only for the most part.

Other kinds of Voidlings existed beside the mindless shadows. These entities had intelligence, purpose, and desire, and were quite dangerous. Anyone who might survive an encounter with such a creature rarely did so intact, or with even a semblance of sanity. The thing that had followed Ethan was of the latter kind—it had to be, given its patience in the courtyard—and had stalked him to me. Clever, really.

I'd give the Voidling the shop, but I'd have to take Ethan into Forget with me, a kinder fate, but not by much. Upstairs, I shrugged into my finest black waistcoat and navy blue necktie. The coat had a custom-made holster stitched into the lining for a six-by-nine paperback. Heading back downstairs, I plucked *Tales of Atlantis*, hidden in plain sight, from one of the piles of books stacked haphazardly on the spiral staircase.

Ethan had helped himself to a sip of spicy Captain's rum in my absence. Good for him. I nodded at a dusty glass, and he poured me two fingers' worth.

"You ready?"

"Ready for what?" he asked.

"We're going to skip a few lessons in your education, Mr. Reilly. But we'll have to act fast. As soon as that thing outside senses a drop of Will from either of us it'll attack, for no other reason than its hunger." My ward enchantments were useless against the Voidling's power, and after all the time away from Forget, I wasn't sure if I still had the strength to fight it.

"Okay, but what about Sophie?"

My first thought was an unkind one. My second, somewhat worse. I had no reason to think she was already dead, not based on the evidence, but with a Voidling on the loose, her chances were slim. Ethan must have read the look on my face. He moaned.

"Sophie can take care of herself," I said.

"I'm not going with you if she's in trouble," he said, swallowing hard. "I came to you for help. But if you're just going to run, then I-I'll find her, by myself."

"That's fine."

"What?"

"Do what you like. Come with me or don't, Ethan. You're more than free to make your own choice—"

There was a pounding on the shop door. I glanced over, startled, and it was my turn to moan. Clare Valentine stood just beyond my invisible ward line, unable or unwilling to cross it without permission. Probably unable. Behind her were a half-dozen grim-faced men and women in long grey cloaks, a retrieval squad of Knights Infernal, unless I missed my guess.

"Who's that?"

"Trouble."

I tapped the book concealed in my coat thoughtfully for a moment. Could I still flee? Of course, but to leave Clare to the Voidling… I wasn't that far gone.

"Go flip the sign over, would you, Ethan."

"What about—?"

"Trust me."

He did as he was told. I knocked aside an ashtray and tiny ceramic pipe atop my sales counter, and then assumed a casual position seated atop it. The *Tales of Atlantis* I slipped from my holster and into a stack of cheap romance paperbacks. To be caught with that, even by Clare, would be to sign my own death warrant.

As soon as the wards were down Clare stepped inside and motioned her six followers to wait outside. She glanced at Ethan, no doubt sensing the sloppy shield around his Will, and moved between Sci-Fi and General Fiction to keep both Ethan and me in view.

"Hello, Declan."

"Hello, Clare."

"You know why I'm here?"

"Of course. I'm to be arrested for breaking the conditions of my exile."

Clare bit her lip. "I'm sorry. Faraday's orders."

"Quite all right, sweet thing." I picked up a tape gun from the counter and held down the flaps on a delivery box. "For what it's worth, I think we've both been set up by powers unseen. No matter. I was just about to pay the faux king a visit, anyway."

"Declan, are you *mad?* Run, run now. Any Knight will arrest you on sight. Christ, that's why I'm here! When we bring you in, Faraday will have you executed. He's forcing you out."

"I got me some bigger problems, Clare."

"Like what?"

I frowned. "Like trying to find the start of this goddamn roll of tape."

"I *said* we should run..." Ethan mumbled, casting nervous glances at the open door.

The Voidling was doing what its kind did best. Waiting in the shadows. As soon as someone used their Will, it would attack and latch onto the energy like two magnets snapping together. At its most powerful, it would feed. The thing that had come to kill me was now my secret weapon... but still Clare's enemy.

"And no, I'm not mad," I said. "Merely tired. Frustrated. Cast aside and discarded. Exiled beyond the Final Vanguards, no? All just for show. To keep the people happy and subdued. Give them someone to hate." I slowly let out my breath. "Clare, there's a Voidling hiding in the courtyard outside."

She blinked. "You're bluffing."

"No."

"No?"

"No," Ethan interjected, and then wished he hadn't when Clare scrutinized him. "I saw it. It followed me here."

"And who are you in all of this?"

"Clare, Ethan. Ethan, Clare. He's got the talent."

One of Clare's entourage stepped into the shop. A tall, grizzled man that reminded me of Marcus. He rested his hand on the pommel of a curved sword concealed by his cloak and glared something akin to pure, crude hatred at me. The crest on his cloak marked him as one of the feared guards of Starhold, the Forgetful prison. I offered him a winning smile.

"What's the delay, Valentine?"

"Arthur," said Clare, "Hale says there's a Voidling in the courtyard."

The big man snorted. "Right. And I'm the next High King of Atlantis. Come off it. He'll say anything. Do you know how unlikely it is a Voidling crossed into True Earth?"

I didn't have to say anything. My new friend Arthur was about to play his part in this impromptu script all too well. He produced a set of star iron manacles, inscribed with runes in the Infernal language. My, my... I warranted the highest honors. Those manacles suppressed Will and placed a blanket of crushing fatigue upon whoever was unlucky enough to wear them.

"Don't try and resist, exile."

"Arthur, wait—" Clare interrupted. Her eyes flashed from emerald green to a fierce and fiery red. She believed me about the Voidling, but it was too late.

Arthur tapped his Will and I did nothing to stop him. The runes on the manacles began to glow. They sprang open at the same instant an unholy and soul-wrenching *screech* reverberated across the courtyard. All of the windows along my storefront imploded in a hail of jagged shrapnel.

I was already moving. As Ethan cursed and Clare dived toward me, I stepped forward and raised a hand against the thousands of tiny missiles. A whispered thought and a cone of ethereal light spread outwards from my palm, creating a shield in front of Ethan, Clare and myself. The rain of deadly glass shards slammed into the wall of force and shattered again, to dust and less than dust.

Arthur wasn't so lucky. He stood beyond my range—and was cut to ribbons. The star iron cuffs fell to the floor.

I laughed.

The force of the Voidling's rage had knocked the majority of Clare's Knights against the front of my shop. They recovered quickly, drawing books and swords bound in lines of pure story. They all looked so young out there, standing well armed but alone against the nightmare hiding in shadow.

"It's after me, I guess." I rubbed my hands together in anticipation. Clare had moved to my side, as she had done so many times in the Tome Wars. She held a small dagger in one hand with a ruby in its hilt—her Infernal Blade—and in the other a small paperback. "You know words are no good against these things."

Clare blinked, swallowed, and then nodded. "Right." She slipped the book away. "What's the plan, Commander?"

I didn't bother to correct her or deny the title.

"Stay out of my way," I said, and meant it. "That goes twice for you, Ethan." I tossed him the bottle of Captain's and he caught it on reflex. "Pay attention, though, sunshine. You may learn something."

A rotten gloominess had descended across Riverwood Plaza as I stepped outside to confront the creature of nightmare. Shadows eclipsed the fountain, and the water that had been clear ran dark and bubbled up and over the rim. The substance wasn't water but thick, living oil—a shadow made real.

The glass had been blown out of all the windows in the courtyard. Terrified civilians scattered every which way, as the creature that had been hiding in the fountain took shape. The Voidling's scream had toppled the frozen banana cart.

Old Mathias was nowhere to be seen, which pissed me off more than anything else so far.

The Knights did not hesitate. As one, they fired blasts of superheated energy into the undulating pool of slick blackness that crept toward my shop. I remained behind them, out of the line of fire. Doing as she was told, Clare stayed behind me.

The Voidling kept on coming, absorbing the flame, the ice, *and* the lightning. These Knights weren't the strongest of the order, not by a long shot.

Then, the Voidling was upon us, blotting out the sun. All sound seemed to die as the Knights fought the terrible thing which grew six, then seven, then eight feet tall. It finally assumed a shape which was vaguely human, a trunk with arms and legs, but where its head should have been was an ugly, rotating sphere of dark oil. The thing had no facial features, yet I felt it look at me. It shrieked again, but the latest noise seemed just a whisper.

Which fractured five minds.

One by one, the Knights slumped. Some fell to their knees, drooling, while others managed a stifled cry before dropping, limp, to the cobblestones. Such was the power of the abstract—of the Void. It had gotten close enough to work its vicious influence and would soon devour not only flesh but souls.

I heard Clare mumbling incoherent nonsense behind me. She gripped my arm, and her eyes, distant and dusty, were the color of old paper. I turned back to the Voidling, pulled myself free of Clare, and stepped in front of the defeated Knights to stand before the creature from beyond space and time.

We regarded one another for a careful moment, and then I plunged my hands into its chest. *Huh… guess you don't forget how to ride a bike.*

It didn't have a face, just that dark orb of oily light, but I thought I caught a momentary flicker of surprise in its form as I gripped its not-heart. *Good*, I thought. *Fear me, you son-of-a-bitch.*

What happened next surprised even me. As I tore its very being asunder, the Voidling *laughed*. It spoke, not aloud, but into my mind.

"Oblivion sees you, Shadowless. Oblivion is watching."

I recoiled, disgusted at its touch inside my head. Its words tasted like rancid milk in the back of my throat. A bolt of wild Will rushed down my arms and burst out of my hands, inside the creature, and flames of emerald light consumed it from within. I turned away at the last moment, just before it exploded, to shield my face from the radiance.

Just like that, the spell was broken. Reality, proper reality, snapped back into place. The sights and sounds of the courtyard, the screams of bystanders, mostly, and the gush of water flooding the plaza from the cracked fountain, came back into stark focus.

Tapping my chin, I pondered the Voidling's words for a moment and then turned back to Clare. She sat within a broken window frame of my shop and held her head in her hands. The Knights strewn on the ground around her mumbled and groaned, which was actually a good sign. Perhaps they had kept their sanity.

Clare gasped as I touched her shoulder. She looked up, pale as a ghost. "How did you do that?" she whispered. "Declan, you *touched* it. Your mind should be soup."

"That's my little secret, sweet thing." Seeing her perplexed expression turn to actual fear, I dropped the pretence. "I got a lot more than I bargained for when I sold my shadow for some magic beans."

Clare stood shakily, holding my forearm for balance. "You can fight them... No, you can do more than that. They don't affect you, do they? If Faraday knew—"

"He'd probably see it as another reason to chop off my head. Remember why you're here today. To wrap me in shackles and deliver me to my execution."

"I was…" Clare shook her head, trying to clear the taste of the Void, no doubt. "That is… I didn't know about the star iron."

"It doesn't matter now, and don't worry, I believe you." I kissed her forehead. "I really was about to deliver myself there, anyway."

"To Ascension City?"

I nodded. "Want to come with me?"

Clare seemed to get a hold on herself and stood up a little straighter. She let go of my arm. "No." She moved over to the nearest fallen Knight and turned her over. The woman stared at the sky unblinking. She'd gnawed a chunk from the flesh of her bottom lip. "I have to tend to my unit. Please, help me."

"Sorry, no. I must be on my way. But I'll send out the work experience kid."

I stepped back into my shop. Ethan stood staring at me with wide eyes. He clutched the bottle of rum hard enough to turn his knuckles white. Other than that, he seemed in good working order.

"Declan," Clare called. I glanced over my shoulder. "Try not to get yourself killed."

No promises.

It was time to go too far.

HOLD ALL SALVOS: PART II

Destiny smells of dust and the libraries of night.
He leaves no footprints.
He casts no shadow.

~ Sandman (Neil Gaiman)

> *A forgetful rose to guide him,*
> *The curse of a madman's last whim.*
> *Crystal petals—blood, bone and steel.*
> *Wrath and ruination brought to heel.*
>
> ~The Historian of Future Prospect
> After Madness, 2007

Wrought, indeed, from words
Rent—torn asunder!
Islands no more, dear
Truth. A pity, you dolt,
Enigmatic fool.

~King Morrow's Journal (Vol. VII)

CHAPTER ELEVEN

Eggshells

The roads to Ascension City, on the very border of the real world—True Earth—and the realms of Forget, were varied and plentiful. *Highways jammed with broken heroes, boss.*

Ascension City could be dived from along the ragged edge of the burning page.

Or I could reach it from a multitude of adjoining realms within Forget itself.

Hell, the city could even be stumbled upon by accident. The home of the Knights Infernal, the last bastion of order and law against the Void, not only brushed up against True Earth, but often times overlapped. Paint on the porous canvas ran, and the lines of reality blurred.

Many a clueless mortal had found their way into Forget and the city purely by elusive thought. The crossover boundaries were, for the most part, fluid and unpredictable. A select few, however, were *always* present. Always and in all ways. The Knights patrolled the ones they knew about, trying in vain to monitor the ebb and flow of citizens through the vast, sprawling metropolis and surrounds.

Easier to hold water in a sieve than secure doorways that spanned not only universes but time. I kept one such doorway upstairs in my bathroom, and although I intended to make myself known to the Knights and King Faraday, the only hope I had of keeping my head would be to return under cloak-and-dagger and ensure past secrets had remained buried these long, short years.

See a man about a sword. See an old friend, perhaps one last time.

Fate seemed to demand that I died in the not-too-distant future, amidst the shards of spilt scotch and unfinished story. Mayhap I was walking that street, and walking it blind, but I'd always been one to act. To sit idly by, to let the Knights and the Voidlings and the Renegades come a knockin' without challenge… Tal would think me such a coward.

So, leaving Clare to clean up the mess downstairs and leaving Ethan to search for Sophie, or perhaps what was left of Sophie, I headed up the spiral staircase, knocking over a stack of heavy Tolstoys in my hurry, slipped under the caution tape, and into my twisted bathroom.

The tomb-dark Black Mirror hung in the air, ugly and ominous. Voidish not-light flowed along the cracks in the wall behind the mirror—flowed *from* the mirror.

Worried about your little world falling apart? whispered a nagging voice in the back of my mind. I stepped in front of the mirror and confronted my lost, my abandoned, my oh-so-broken shadow.

The pale reflection's grin revealed two rows of jagged yellow teeth. His time through the looking glass had not been kind. He offered me his hand. Surely he must know full well that the clock, which had started ticking years ago, had finally counted down to zero. A buzz of static tension crackled through the air.

I sighed and plunged my arm, up to the elbow, in the inky glass. My limb slipped through the mirror, and needles of freezing ice lit every nerve under my skin on fire. My reflection seemed stunned for only the briefest of moments. Perhaps stunned that I had actually done it. Then his grin turned feral and nasty, and he grasped my arm with his own, digging his filthy fingernails into my flesh.

He pulled me from my feet and out of reality—into the Void.

Even with a mind trained and forged into steel at the Infernal Academy, my crossing into the space between universes wholly, and for any period of time, was to invite madness. Lucky for me, I'd done this before. If I played the game, kept my sanity, I would emerge from the Void within reach of Ascension City, given where the Black Mirror had been cast just before my exile.

The old rundown bathroom disappeared. Pitch-blackness wrapped itself around the inverted space. I stood in something thick and viscous—oil, of the kind that had spawned the Voidling in the courtyard back in Perth.

"Nothing for it," I whispered. The words echoed out over the vast, endless space. For all that mattered, I was gazing at infinity, in every dark direction. Of my feral shadow, the surly reflection in the Black Mirror, there was no sign.

I trudged through the knee-high oil. The going was slow and tiresome as if I was wading in treacle. I soon panted from the exertion and wondered vaguely what substance I was breathing. It sure as shit wasn't air, not in this place.

Best to think of it as a corridor, Aloysius Jade whispered from the past. Before being sentenced to life in Starhold for genocide, Jade had been one of the chief instructors at the Academy. He was perhaps Forget's foremost expert on navigating the Void cold. *A hallway from A to B. Just concentrate on where you're heading and the link will pull you through.*

Well, my link was five years old—and tenuous at best. But the mirror was all I had, despite the danger in the Void. A prickling sensation on the back of the neck told me I was being watched. Or paranoid. Was my elusive shadow, forfeited in Atlantis to an old god and made sentient, out for revenge?

I could still feel its corpse-like fingers on my forearm which made me think of bones, of laughing skulls rattling in dank, dirty seawater, coated in slimy seaweed, the water hued pale green under a starless night sky.

"Damn, should've brought a bottle of something triple distilled…"

The Void was a place of mindless and violent chaos, overseen by a ruling class of viciously intelligent beings. *And at least one god.* Atlantis had taught me that the hard way on the eve of the Degradation. I probably wasn't just being paranoid, thinking the atmosphere around me too quiet. Something should have at least tried to eat my face by now.

The feeling of being watched hadn't gone away. If anything, I could feel dozens of unseen eyes in the darkness, staring at me, but only staring, watching. Keeping me on course? Was I being given safe passage? That was an odd thought—mad, even. Perhaps the Void had stripped my mind, and I'd been wandering for days. Saner to think I'd been robbed of my sanity than to think the creatures living here wanted me to reach Forget unchallenged.

Something wasn't right, of that I was sure. Add to the equation, the unseen puzzle: the Voidling outside my shop, Clare and her Knights coming to arrest me, my untimely death, the Pagemaster's attack… Well, I didn't know what everything added up to, but I was being driven back to Ascension City, like a pig to slaughter.

Some uncertain amount of time passed as I waded, lost in thought, through the dark oil. Minutes that could have been hours, that could have been days. I felt I was making no progress at all, perhaps only going in circles.

A heartbeat later I walked, face-first, into a wall.

"Ow." A trickle of blood ran from my nose and sizzled as it hit the Void oil, which burned away the life in the red drops. I reached out blindly and ran my hands across the object in my path. After a minute, I realized it was just the outer shell of all creation. *On the outside lookin' in.*

I'd arrived at my destination. *Wastelands treatin' me good.* I placed a hand flat against the wall, which was wet, but not with oil, and muttered a quick invocation of Will. Silver light blazed between my fingers, and for one awful, harrowing moment I lit up the Void.

There were hundreds—thousands—of monstrous creatures surrounding me. The silence was shattered as they screeched against the pure, raw power flowing from my hand, power that was the antithesis of all that they were. Power that could *feed* them. The wall cracked, and reality flooded through the tear—literally.

A torrent of freezing water slammed into me and knocked me back. My Will, a lifeline in the darkness, shot through the gushing flood and pulled me forward.

I was squeezed and pushed body, mind, and soul, through the crack in the wall. Pressed from all sides, I could neither see nor draw breath. The invisible world began to spin, and I tumbled down, down, down until dizzy nausea replaced the squeezing—overpowered it—and I broke through something webbed, like passing through a mesh screen, or breaking out of a barbed net.

It felt like leaving the Void.

I was deep underwater when all my senses kicked back into action. I hadn't planned on emerging somewhere without air. The light was dull, *but there was light,* shimmering away to my left. A soundless scream emerged from my mouth in a rush of bubbles which surged toward the light—toward the surface!

Disoriented, I righted myself and began to claw my way up to breach the surface. My chest felt like a balloon about to burst. A distant, dreary thought of drowning found prominence in my mind. Still, survival was in the cards. I thrust my arms up and down in wild strokes, kicking with the last of my strength. *Just a few more strokes…*

My vision faded, and pretty damn soon I was going to have to draw breath, underwater or not. In some vague, unimportant corner of my head I realized that the water all about me was fresh. A split second before I sucked down a mouthful of otherworldly water, I breached the surface, gasping, and reared up out of the deep pool in a spray of droplets. I gulped the fresh, clear air of Forget.

I fell back down, utterly spent—but alive.

Narrow beams of sunlight cut through a thick forest canopy, overhead. I soaked up the warmth as I floated on my back in the pool. Washing the stink of the Void from my mind and soul would take a long time, more time than I probably had left.

I laughed. There was no mistaking the large, twisted trees or the scent of Will on the air. "I'm back..." On my own head be it, exile or not, I was *home*. And what next? Well, in Ascension City they say, my small heart grew three sizes that day.

A waterfall splashed down slick stones above my head, and a green cliff face stretched up above the roof of the forest beyond that. I turned in the water, looking for a way onto dry land.

Across the way, a young girl with a friendly face waved at me from the shoreline. She sat on the water's edge, dangling her thin, pale legs in the pool.

"Good afternoon, Declan Hale," the Historian of Future Prospect said. "You're late, you're late, for a very important date."

CHAPTER TWELVE

Ascension City

"You knew I'd be coming through here?" That was a stupid question to ask someone who saw every possible future, burning through her mind in lines of verse, but the Historian still offered me a kind smile. "No, of course you did. I'm sorry. Call me a little out of practice dealing with the wonders of Forget."

She pulled her feet out of the water and stood up. The sunlight filtering through the canopy overhead glittered in her silver hair which sparkled like diamonds. Atop her head, she wore a net of spun gold. "I wanted to see you for myself. The man who sold the world."

I swam to the shore. "We've met before. Once. You were just a wee little thing. Four feet and change."

"Yes, I remember." The Historian pressed her fingers against her forehead, as if the memory pained her. "A long time ago. Before you became… shadowless."

I pulled myself up out of the pool and sat down on a mossy boulder next to the girl, but not too close. She was one of the most important, and most protected, people in all of Forget. I had an inkling there were concealed bodyguards all around, waiting for me to make an unwise move. Her shadow stretched out from our shared boulder, along the shores of the pool. Mine did not.

"All things being even, not so long ago, really."

The Historian placed a hand on my knee, and I tensed. Slivers of light danced between her fingers. Hot air rushed up beneath my waistcoat and down my trousers. She dried my clothes and left me feeling all warm and fuzzy. Perhaps there weren't any bodyguards, after all. In that brief moment, I'd sensed a Will as vast and as strong as… as… Wow, I had no words for it.

She was power incarnate.

"You do not seem surprised to see me, Declan Hale."

"To be honest, kid, very little surprises me. I died this week, you know."

"Yes, I know. I *Saw*." She frowned. "Or rather, I saw the events *around* you. As you are now—without shadow—my Sight glances over you."

I paused. "Am I still on that path?"

"Aren't we all?" She raised a single eyebrow and chuckled. "But yes, I know what you mean. You have about four days before you die."

"Anything I can do to avoid that?"

Her gaze was soft, always kind, but I sensed a piercing disappointment directed my way, nonetheless. "That's a nice waistcoat, Declan, but you must see that it's not about redemption anymore. You long ago forfeited any right to that."

I shrugged. "Suppose I did."

"Only Tal Levy can forgive you your past, at least when it comes to the cost of the Degradation. The *true* cost. The one you keep hidden. The rest is up to you."

"Tal's dead. Ash in the wind, Miss Prospect. You can see the future, all that will ever be, but you forget what's already been."

"I see you embracing her before your death. Now, then, and soon is all relative."

"Is this what you came to tell me? Why you had to see me for yourself?"

"No." She stood up on her bare feet, straightening her purple skirts. The Historian was a cute little thing—with the accumulated strength of ages-to-come coursing through her mind. "I am here to tell you to be brave. That you are going to have to be brave."

"Is that a riddle, or some such cryptic nonsense? If there's something I need to know, kid, then tell me now— plainly."

"That's against the rules, as much as glimpses of vast and multiple futures can have rules."

"Are you trying to tell me I don't have to die?"

She shook her head. "All the futures I see end in your death. Five days, Declan Hale. Five days to make your peace and find your forgiveness."

"Gee, I'm awful glad you stopped by with such good news. I came here to change that fate." I held my head and thought of what waited on the other side of this forest. The city. The past. All the king's horsemen vying for my head... "They think killing me will make their problems go away— that my death will somehow undo the damage. It will not."

But never mind. I'd chosen to return, to see what my death was all about.

I stopped feeling sorry for myself and concentrated on harnessing a resolve that would see me through. "I can't imagine this is easy for you. Being here. Why did you really want to see me?"

The Historian shrugged and, for just a moment, looked like the sixteen-year-old girl she was supposed to be— innocent and uncertain. "Because you're..." She grasped at the air, looking for the words. "Before the end, you're going to be given a chance, a moment in time... to do something that no one has ever done before."

"Oh?"

"Yes, that's as close as I can See it. Something *new*. Something… of absurd importance. You, Declan Hale—the Shadowless Arbiter—are going to hold infinity in the palm of your hand, and eternity in an hour."

"You're quoting Blake." I scraped a chunk of moss from the boulder. "Fitting, I suppose. And then I die?"

"Yes, and then you die."

"Yay."

The Historian stepped away from me. She clasped her hands together over her breasts, and the blue sapphire hanging around her neck shone with a soft, ethereal light. As I had done seven years ago, during my graduation at the Infernal Academy, I fell to one knee before her. Back then we had been the same height, even while I was on my knees. Now my head was level with her waist. She placed a gentle hand on my short, tousled hair.

"The next few days are going to hurt, Declan."

"I know."

"Your enemies are not all evil."

"I know."

"You should forgive Jon Faraday."

"I know. But never."

A single tear traced a lonely track down the Historian's cheek. She let it fall unchecked, and without thought, I reached out my open palm and caught it. That brought a smile back to her face.

"When we first met, I feared you, Declan. You scared me so much. More than the old Knights, the battle-scarred veterans, or all the dark tales of Renegade cruelty put together. Do you know why?"

"Of course." I couldn't keep my voice from wavering, just a little. "Because of the future—or the past, now. You Saw what I was going to do. What I would become. Atlantis, the war's end. The Degradation unleashed and the Story Thread crippled. Reach City and all who lived there destroyed. I wish you'd told me some of it, at least enough to save Tal. Or enough… to die in her place."

"No, that's not why. Never mind." She folded her hands over an elaborate belt, studded with gemstones. "You hated me after you were exiled."

"Yes."

"And now?"

I sighed. "Why shoot the messenger? Laws and accords as old as the universe itself bind you. It's not fair, but that's life, right? Various shades of not-fair and regret." I kissed the back of the Historian's hand and stood, having paid homage long enough. "That's a good thing, I suppose. If life were fair, then all these bad things that happen to us would be because we deserved them."

"Declan... you take cake, okay."

Old jokes again. She really did see everything. "Don't you mean take care?"

"That too."

~~*~*

I'd travelled into Forget and the realm of Ascension City unassisted and untethered to the real world. No book or written word had brought me across universes.

I was here in truth, having survived the Void with sanity intact. I could not float back to Perth on a whim.

Coming through the Void put me at a disadvantage. The only way back was across the Void again or through one of the guarded gates, where Forget and True Earth overlapped. If I was taken prisoner in the city—and I would be—I would have no easy way of escape. I'd have to rely on my charm and a winning attitude if I was going to survive. Yeah, that would see me through. *S'all gravy, baby.*

The path through the forest was paved with old cracked stones, worn and weathered. Bristly tufts of grass and fat vines grew between the slabs and crept along the soil banks on either side of the green corridor. I followed the path north, tasting the wind. Overhead, unseen through the canopy, I could hear the rumbling of airships flying toward the city.

"Good to be back," I reminded myself. "Oh, yes indeedy."

The Historian had abandoned me by the pool. She had used a leather-bound tome to slip back to her temple in the mountains to the east of Ascension City. Once I watched her disappear, I remembered I'd left *Tales of Atlantis* back on the counter in my bookshop. That was sloppy. I had a feeling I was going to need it, before all was said and done.

I followed the path for a few miles, winding through the trees and thinking deep thoughts. My polished black shoes were soon scuffed and biting at my ankles. They weren't made for strolling in the woods. *What other way into the universe, though, Muir?*

The path meandered alongside a river too wide to cross. I skirted the banks and headed as north as I could manage. The cobbled, broken stone and overgrown weeds were dwindling. The canopy had receded, too, and I beheld the late afternoon sky overhead. Tiny zipping dots, cruisers and ships, darted to and fro within the clouds. Ascension City drew close now, and my whole returning-to-the-scene-of-the-crime lark began to seem very real. The trees had thinned enough that I could glimpse the edge of the forest.

Ten minutes later, I emerged from the tree line on the crest of a tall hill. From that vantage point, I beheld my old stomping grounds with a mix of wearied relief and rising trepidation.

"Oh, you pretty thing," I muttered.

I'd sensed home before I'd seen it. Ascension City housed tens of millions of people. Hundreds of thousands of those were gifted with Will, low-level practitioners, for the most part, who could do little more than light a candle. Other inhabitants fell into the intermediate crowd, who usually couldn't pass the Academy's brutal entrance examinations but were suited to enchantment and augmentation work. As for the upper class, the experts, I could sense one or two flares of power on par with the Knights Infernal.

The city looked magnificent.

Modern architecture and ancient design came into relief against a backdrop of darkening sky. Ascension City appeared beyond its time and wouldn't have looked out of place in an epic Sci-Fi novel set on an alien world. The buildings were futuristic, yet to the east, large swaths were charred and under construction. *Reconstruction.* Half a decade had passed since I'd left, and most of the damage I'd wrought had yet to be repaired.

But the lights were on, and the roads and skies were heavy with traffic. I guessed the city thrived.

Mighty towers, almost wreathed in clouds, scraped at the sky. Glass domes extended over stadium-sized fields, and walkways stretched from the peak of one building to the next—bridges built in the air over the city. Neon-blue lighting ran up and down the streets and throughout hundreds of the buildings. Its energy came from the conduit of tapped power running beneath the city, a font of true power from the heart of creation, bleeding through a crack in the canvas of reality.

The near-eternal source of energy powered the intricate grid and had kept the city running even during the most strenuous hours of the old wars.

Although most inhabitants didn't know it, Ascension City was a poor imitation of Atlantis.

One tower rose above all others in the heart of the city and shone like a beacon in the half-light, a white spire of pure obsidian stone, monolithic and imposing. Even at this distance, I could see the unnatural smoothness of the rock, the polished finish and metal trim. Blue lights ran up the tower in a spiral pattern, and a single white sphere of fire, at the tower's peak, ignited a flat plateau.

The Fae Palace of the Knights Infernal had been carved from a mountain long centuries ago. The heart of the city was the crystal core of a mountain long dead. The rest of

Ascension City, some thirty miles across, sprawled out from that central tower.

I had missed this place.

~~*~*

I made no effort to mask my appearance as I treaded once more familiar paths through the outskirts of the city.

My journey through the Void had spat me out in the forest bordering the south side of town. Emerging in that location was useful. My current destination, the Cedar Sky—a charming old shop in the market district—was only a half hour's walk.

The cobblestone lanes and vaulted stone archways marked the way into the sprawling market area. Contemporary hotels and rustic old inns stood side by side and thrust their upper stories above ramshackle shops. Red-and-white-pebbled bricks lined wide boulevards, which in turn were circled by low hills. The city had been built around those hills.

Crowds of Forgetful citizens—men, women, and children born and raised in this world—meandered in the busy streets. Wheelless taxi-cycles, hovering a foot above the ground, zoomed down roadways alongside old wooden carts. Ascension City was a blur of the past, present, and future. With so many conflicting realms, it was impossible for anyone to keep time in order. The city may have been ultramodern in part, by standards back in the real world, but its people and customs spanned five thousand years.

An old farmer selling sticky mangoes the size of soccer balls eyed me warily as I paused on a street corner to wipe the sweat from my brow. "Broken quill, but I know you, don't I, son?"

"Me? No, I don't think so." Best to avoid a riot so early in the game.

I moved on, leaving the old man wagging his finger at me and tapping his head. I made it a few shops down the lane before his startled cry cut through the air. "Hale! By the Everlasting, that was Declan Hale!"

Bugger…

Murmurs and shocked whispers rippled through the throngs of Forgetfuls, putting me in the calm heart of a swirling tornado. In a city of people from all corners of Forget, skins dark or pale, clothes of bright and strange cut, faces masked or hair dyed violent colors, *I* was the one that stood out like a sore thumb, a record skipping a beat—*sing it true, songbird*—or a cat hunting among the pigeons. Five years ago, and I imagine even in the years since, my face had been plastered on every wall and screen for a hundred worlds.

"On a steel horse I ride…" *Wanted: Dead or Alive.*

The crowds parted for me, the infamous exiled Knight, and I strolled through lanes and enjoyed the freedom offered by my pseudo-celebrity. That freedom would all come crashing down soon, I was sure. The soft, pleasant aroma of turmeric and a thousand other spices, teas, and seeds wafted on the air as I headed deeper into the quarter. I was nearly at my destination but kept my eyes peeled for trouble.

I could easily imagine a dagger in the back or a bullet to the brain, not to mention attacks of a more supernatural nature. Strands of silver light trailed behind me from my clenched fists. My Will was alight, daring anyone to try and stop me.

None dared.

A few minutes later, followed by hordes of grim-faced men but so far unmolested, I reached the storefront and home of an old friend. Barrels of cashew nuts, pistachios, and red dates sat out front of the Cedar Sky. Exotic teas and coffees in canvas bags were stacked thirty feet high against the crooked, fieldstone building.

Whistling a merry tune, I let myself in.

Inside was hot and humid. Wiry, Byzantine folk music wailed from an old gramophone. More barrels and satchels of herbs were scattered atop buckled wooden tables. Scents of wolfberry and ginseng hung in the air. That smell, more than anything else so far, made me realize just where I was and how far I'd travelled since breakfast that morning.

"Welcome, welcome," chimed a deep, cheerful voice from somewhere behind the immense stocks of earthy produce. "Welcome to Cedar Sky. How may I—?" The voice emerged from behind a wall of herbs before it cut off abruptly.

"Aaron!" I pointed a finger at the portly man. "Long time no—"

"No!" Aaron backed away and fell over his chair. He hit the floor with a solid thud which rattled the various alchemical bottles on the shelves. "Oh sweet, broken quill—no, no, *no*. Not now, not ever. Hale, get out of here! You insane bastard—did anyone see you enter this shop?"

"No."

"Well, praise Allah for small—"

"*Everyone* saw me come in here."

Aaron hauled himself up, his pale face splotched with high spots of red, and whimpered. "Then we are both dead men."

"You're not even a little bit happy to see me?"

"Ha!" He shuffled around his shop while he wrung his hands and laughed nervously. "Happy to see you? I'd convinced myself you were dead. You may as well have been. Declan Hale, the harbinger of Degradation itself, exiled from Forget forever under pain of death—and for any who would dare stand with him! No, Hale, no. I am not happy to see you."

"Give me a hug, big guy."

Aaron ceased his shuffling and exhaled a long burst of air—the sigh of the long suffering. He took a moment to try to compose himself and then burst into tears. "I always knew I'd see you again, in this life or the next." He wrapped his thick, bear-like arms around me and squeezed. He smelt like Old Spice—wood shavings, sawdust, and probably the 1960s all rolled into one. "You won't live another day, but it is good to see you."

"Do you still have the chest I left?"

"Of course I do. And I know what's in it, too."

"You didn't open—?"

"No, I did not. But it started *growing*, Declan. I spend half my week gardening in the basement of the villa on Lake Delgado because of that damn thing. White roses, everywhere! Everlasting save me, I wouldn't dare open it."

"Well, all good then. Not that you could use it, but it's a relief to know no one else has either." I tapped my chin. "After all, who's going to look for Forget's greatest treasure in your basement?"

~~*~*

Aaron and I did not have to wait long. Just long enough to become reacquainted. The years fell away, as they only could with old friends. We shared a cup of honeyed tea and savored the calm before the storm.

No more than fifteen minutes into my surprise visit, we were descended upon by what was possibly every Knight in the city. Ten squads of ten, a hundred adept men and women, looking resplendent in their dress uniforms, filled the street outside. Five older Knights, veterans of the Tome Wars with medals on their chests to prove it, barged into the store with Infernal blades drawn and expressions of forbidding death on their faces... and a little something that might have been fear.

I was placed under arrest—hands bound behind my back with metal cuffs and everything. Aaron was ordered to accompany me and the Knights. He remained unrestrained but no longer as free as he'd been a quarter hour ago. Surrounded by the guard, smoky trails of luminescent silver light cupped in every one of their palms, I was marched through the streets. Half the squad ran ahead and cleared the way to a waiting... machine. Well, the object looked like a helicopter without the blades, and it hovered a few inches from the ground, in a wide plaza at the end of the row.

On closer inspection, I knew it to be a troop carrier, fitted with fusion engines, capable of swift, low-altitude flight. I was familiar with the older models that had been used in the wars, contraptions held together with duct tape and good intentions. The carrier in front of me looked to be a newer model—flashier. Jon Faraday had been disturbingly busy.

Oh well, I suppose Ascension City was nice from above.

We took flight and hastily cut a track through the air, toward the monolithic palace in the centre of town. The skyways must have been cleared in advance for us, for the ride was a smooth, uninterrupted run over the maze of streets below.

"You know they're probably burning my shop to the ground right now," Aaron said, rather glumly. "You couldn't wait until nightfall, could you, Declan? Snuck back under the cover of darkness? Oh no, no, no. Not you, not Declan *bloody* Hale."

I chuckled. "You know I own a shop myself these days, back on Earth."

Aaron blinked. "Oh?"

"I sell books."

He opened and closed his mouth a few times, like a goldfish bobbing for air. "That is… absurd. Are you intentionally trying to piss off King Faraday?"

"Quiet," grumbled one of the grizzled old Knights. He had a slick, nasty-looking revolver rested on his knee and pointed at my heart. "One more word, Hale. Just one."

We landed on the very summit of the palace, a mile above the city, on a helipad next to a twenty-foot-high flaming torch of white light. The Knights spilled out of the cruiser, then clustered themselves around Aaron and me. We didn't so much walk as were dragged across the landing pad and into a large, lavish elevator cut into the side of the obsidian stone. At this point most of the guard left us, save for the five older Knights who had stormed Aaron's shop.

The elevator was a tight fit. We descended one hundred floors, entirely bypassing the throne room, the courts, and the Academy levels of the palace. If memory served me, and it did, we were being escorted to the suite levels close to the ground floor. The doors *binged* open and revealed a hallway that would not have looked out of place in a five-star hotel.

One could almost forget one was in a mile-high palace carved from a single piece of mountainous stone.

I wasn't thrown into a dark and dank cell, which was something, but a cage is a cage is a cage. Aloysius Jade would have had something to say on the matter, I was sure. Aaron and I were shown to separate rooms. He cast an unhappy glance over his shoulder and disappeared around a bend in the tower.

"Sit," ordered my revolver-wielding guard, once I was tucked away in my room. I sat. "Your restraints should be along shortly."

The guard stayed with me until a set of shiny star cuffs were brought up from the Collections. While we waited, his two lackeys stripped and searched me—thoroughly.

"Any one of you handsome bastards could've bought me dinner first," I quipped.

My clothes were seized. Standing naked and unashamed, my body a roadmap of old scars, I didn't resist the Will suppressing manacles as they closed around my wrists, but I did begrudge how tight they were drawn.

Then the guards withdrew, locking the heavy wooden door behind them. None of them had spoken more than two words to me. Orders against it, most likely. A pitcher of cool water sat on the dresser, across from a large double bed. I poured myself a glass and turned to the large square window, which offered a twilit sky and an impressive view of Ascension City.

I let out a long, slow breath. I was back—home, for all that mattered, breathing the air of my favorite world once more. I retrieved a towel from the en suite bathroom and wrapped it around my waist with some difficulty, given the restraints. The star cuffs sapped my strength and blanketed me in a shroud of fatigue. I tried to conjure a ball of pure energy but couldn't. Well, no sense in fighting the weariness. After the day I'd had, the bed looked more than inviting.

I was asleep as soon as my head hit the pillow.

That night I dreamed of Tal and distant stars. She stole my shadow, wrapped it in light, and cast it spinning across the Void. *'Oblivion is watching…'* she whispered. Her eyes were the color of heart's blood.

CHAPTER THIRTEEN

Punk in Drublic

I awoke with a strangled start just after two in the morning, according to the clock on the wall. Days and nights here in Forget mirrored the cycle back on Earth. My mind was foggy and dull, and I struggled to sit up. The cuffs pressed their diabolical runes against my flesh, locked the door to my Will, and left me feeling as if I hadn't slept at all.

Yawning, I fell back and decided a few more hours' rest was priority *uno*.

Something bright exploded just outside the window. *Fireworks*, I thought dully. The spinning wheel of color grew until it eclipsed the night sky. *Wait...*

A blast shattered my window in an impressive display of electric-blue lightning and orange fire. The impact sent me hurtling ass-over-head across the bed and onto the floor.

Needless to say, half a heartbeat later I was wide awake and on my feet, diving for cover. The towel fell from my waist, and I stood behind an armchair, as naked as the day I was born.

Two creatures of Forgetful hell's spawn, pulled straight from old nightmares—or, more likely, from the Degradation—stood on the writing desk by the window. Flames licked at the polished oak and blazed across the walls and carpet.

"Hello, boys," I snarled, flexing the star cuffs. If I broke my thumbs perhaps I could slip free…

Both demons folded identical pairs of near-transparent wings into the thick, rotten hide on their backs. They were thin creatures, of wasted leathery skin stretched over elongated bones. The grey skin around their mouths pulled tautly across two rows of sharp fangs which dripped viscous yellow pus. It stank to high-heaven, and I was across the room.

"Your betrayal ends tonight, Hale," said the one on my left, Tweedledum. Its voice was worse than screeching harpies. The sound ran down my spine.

I scoffed. During the height of the Tome Wars, I'd wiped the floor with demonic dipshits twice as ugly as these two. Will or not, I was unafraid.

Tweedledee roared, its grip tightening around a familiar sword. The hilt was wrapped in leather, the blade sharp, cruelly curved, and imbued with unknown enchanted strengths. I'd burnt a layer of flesh off my hand once, touching a sword like that.

"Calm down," I said, somewhat reasonably. Smoke gathered in the air as the flames consumed the walls. "Who, or what, sent you?"

Two pairs of eyes, lifeless black orbs, stared at me with what could have been mirth, if the matching grins that stretched their jaws even wider were any indication. Small spirals of dead Void light shone within those orbs.

"We were sent by one who has taken you seriously."

I took a few slow steps away from the corner of the room, toward the door. Both demons tensed as if they were about to strike. Despite my best efforts, my damned thumbs wouldn't snap. The door had to be locked—I was a prisoner, after all. Where were my jailers?

"Give me a name so I know who to track down and gut like a fish."

"You have been judged accountable, Shadowless."

That was about as useful as a... "You know what? I don't even care." I raised my voice. "I sure hope that the Knights guarding my room don't come in here anytime soon!"

Nothing. *Nada.*

The smoke finally triggered the fire alarms, and the sprinklers overhead burst to life in a rain of cold water accompanied by a piercing siren. Perfect.

I saw my chance. I turned and ran at the door and, wonder of wonders, the knob turned in my hand. Dripping wet and without a towel, I threw the door open as if my life depended on it and *hurled* myself into the hallway.

Anticipating the worst I stayed low, which saved my life as bolts of blue fire *punched* through the wall in a spray of plaster and wood, striking with all the ferocity of a lightning storm. Shrieks rose in untamed fury from within the room and drowned even the fire alarm.

Tweedledum and Tweedledee were going for the kill. They were slower than I thought they'd be, but I decided that was good and not to question what little good fortune came my way. The energy coursed through the wall, setting alight the hallway and blowing to bits various pieces of furniture, flower vases, and hanging paintings.

I stumbled forward, tripped over a handful of corpses, and fell flat on my face.

The Knights guarding my room had been slaughtered, which explained their lack of reaction to my distress call and the explosions. The bodies were warm, the throats slit only minutes ago. Whoever had done it hadn't hung around. Was I dealing with an enemy or a misguided ally? Who had unlocked my room?

I was less than a day back in town and already three dead.

I scuttled across the carpeted floor on my elbows and knees. A steady rain from the sprinklers chilled my bare skin as bolt after bolt of sizzling energy threatened to run me through. Miraculously, I avoided death-by-lightning and rose shakily to my feet, having cleared the edge of the storm.

What's the plan, Dec? Options were somewhat limited. *Run. Run quickly.*

Other palace guests were emerging from their rooms. Blurry eyes heavy with sleep opened up wide as I ran past, naked. No sign of Aaron. I was about halfway to the elevators when behind me my room exploded in a deadly barrage of flying shrapnel. Tweedledum and Tweedledee emerged from within the dust and the flames, wailing for my head.

Fighting the fatigue, I reached the elevator and slammed my fist into the call button, hoping and praying the car wasn't a hundred floors above me. The thin chain of the star cuffs bounced back and forth, perilously close to my manhood. I held up my arms to avoid any debilitating mishaps.

I ducked as the demons raised their swords, and blue fire curled around the dark blades before erupting in half a dozen streaks of vicious, crackling power. The palace guests caught in the hall either cried out or stood stock-still, probably in shock. The lances of hot fire that rent the air had them diving back into their rooms for cover and ignoring the fire alarms.

The elevator doors behind me *binged* open as the wild torrents of electric-flame screamed down the hall. I jumped through the doors and slammed my fist against the button with the two inward-facing arrows. The doors started to close but just a fraction too slow.

Shit! Two wild bolts slipped between the narrow gap in the doors, exploded against the back of the lift, and blasted a hole through to the darkness of the shaft beyond. I threw myself at the carpeted floor. If I'd still been standing, they would've pierced me through the neck and heart.

The button for the ground floor was already aglow as the lift jerked into downward motion. I remembered to breathe as the heavy sound of things exploding above, on my floor, became muffled and ominous.

I stood, took another deep breath, and noticed that I wasn't alone in the lift. I exhaled slowly, staring at a woman who wore a form-hugging red dress and a white porcelain mask. Her dress revealed a remarkable amount of cleavage but covered the rest of her body from head to toe, save her tanned arms. Even her hair was wrapped in a silky satiny hood. She stared at me from behind the mask, then at the smoldering holes in the back of the lift, and then back at me and down at my...

"Um... it's cold out," I said. I was dripping wet, shivering, and bleeding from half a dozen small cuts that I could see. Sounds of wrenching metal echoed up above in the elevator shaft. *Uh-oh.*

"Well, is this awkward, or what?" I asked and strategically held the star cuffs in front of myself. Was that *Born to Run* playing over the speakers in the elevator? The song was a little drowned out by the fire alarm. Something important was nagging at my thoughts, something out of place.

"My name's Declan and I'm to be executed later on today," I said. *No, that wasn't it...*

The lady in red was saved from responding to me, the unclothed lunatic, as the entire elevator *lurched* to the right, slamming us both against the wall. The sound of the heavy whip-crack of taut cable unraveling snapped in the shaft above us.

"Ah hell..." The cable must have broken because the box plummeted down the tunnel. The fall was short and ended quite abruptly, and the woman next to me screamed loud enough to wake the dead. We'd fallen about fifteen feet, I thought, and bounced off the walls to hit the base of the shaft hard enough to jar my shoulders into numbness.

Fucking demons.

For a wonder, the elevator doors *binged* open on the ground floor. I extracted myself from around the lady in red and crawled out of the lift as half a ton of steel cable crashed down upon it, crushing it. Fortunately, the woman had scampered out after me, shaken and somewhat out of sorts—another innocent bystander scarred for life.

"Still alive down here!" I shouted back up the shaft. I was *furious*. A thick column of flame, hot as the blazing sun, burst through the roof of the lift and ignited the tunnel with all the fires of hell.

"Time to go," I said, stifling another yawn—the cuffs were still working their infernal curse upon me, trying to force me to sleep. Adrenalin alone kept me mobile now. I turned away from the burning elevator and beheld the grand palace vestibule, a lavish space of cool marble columns, hung with tapestries and the purple standard of the Dragon Throne.

A small dagger took me just beneath my arm. I felt the cool metal ricochet off my lower ribcage, digging a deep furrow in my side.

I gasped in surprise, in confusion, *in sheer pain*. The lady in red!

My blood, hot and sticky, flowed down the elegant knife in her perfectly manicured hand and across her fingernails. A steady trickle ran over her soft skin down to her elbow. I stood motionless and caught, bent to the side on reflex alone, trying to edge the knife out of my flesh.

"Ow..."

"Hush, hush, sweet Declan," said the murderous woman, her blue eyes truly compassionate behind that white mask. She no longer looked like an innocent bystander, and I was a fool to have been taken in so easily. "It's okay."

"I... thought you were cool."

She leaned in close. I caught the light scent of an unfamiliar fragrance. Lavender, I thought, or perhaps not. She lifted her mask, just enough to reveal her mouth. Her lips, naturally full and red, pressed against mine in a warm kiss that only served to dig the dagger half an inch deeper. I moaned, yet cold surprise hit me harder than the pain.

Breaking the kiss, the lady in red slipped the knife out of me. My legs buckled, failed of all strength, and I fell back onto the smooth velvet carpet. I lifted my head and glanced at my side. Everything was far too crimson.

I don't die here. The thought was not as comforting as I'd hoped.

I sucked in a harsh breath and forced a fresh spurt of blood from the wound, which almost made me chuckle. I grinned at the masked mystery woman who had just stabbed me and kissed me in the same breath.

"Do you think we'll be in love forever?" I asked.

Those luscious red lips, all I had of her, smiled. "Oh my, charming to the last. She never told me how much fun you would be."

"Who...?"

"Now that would be telling, handsome."

Joined by her demonic escort, Tweedledum and Tweedledee, the lady in red blew me another kiss. Of course they were all working together.

Tweedledum and Tweedledee had driven me into her arms, I realized. Escaping them had been too easy. If they'd really been trying to kill me I wouldn't have made it out of my room upstairs. The lady in red drew a slim paperback from inside the folds of her dress. The demons at her side grasped her arms, and together they shimmered and disappeared—off to worlds unknown, unseen, unfound.

She had the talent, then, a Will and the skill to use it. So red lips, a rather impressive chest, and command of the one true power—should be enough information for me to track her down, if I lived.

I tried to sit up. Bad idea.

Either the forced fatigue or the blood loss, or a bitter, lethal cocktail of both, was hampering my vision. I stopped fighting and closed my eyes.

All thoughts faded to black.

CHAPTER FOURTEEN

Strawberry Fields Forever

I awoke in a shaft of sunlight to someone removing my star cuffs. The hum of my Will poured over the dam in my mind. The feeling was invigorating, like being doused with ice water, but it amplified tenfold the burning in my side. Groaning, I tried to roll over, but a firm hand held me in place.

"Of all the places. In all of the realms. Across all of the worlds..." Marcus tossed the cuffs aside, glaring at them as if they were hissing snakes. "You had to come back here."

I was groggy, but my memory was sharp. A memory of lying naked and slowly bleeding to death in the grand vestibule of the Fae Palace, as a woman with luscious red lips looked on. Since then, at least someone had lent me their trousers.

"I hope you're not here to break me out or anything equally as stupid."

Marcus stepped away, and I could see more of the room beyond him which looked exactly like the one that Tweedledum and Tweedledee had incinerated the night before. A familiar man from my past stood opposite Marc, and two men stood in the doorway—Knights Infernal.

"Faraday let me in to see you," said the man near Marc. "He knows you can't run—not this time."

"Aye, he's got that right. Hello, Fenton Creed."

"Hale." Stooping next to me, Fenton peeled away the bandages at my side. "Keep still while I check your stitches. You're not to die just yet—not before your summons at noon."

"Can't you just heal me?"

Fenton smirked. "I *could*." He was tall, rake-thin, and rather unintimidating at first glance. Also at second and third glance. But he possessed the strongest known Will in Forget. His frame belied the fact that he could incinerate legions with his mind. If it came down to a direct battle of Will with him, I would be wiped from existence, smashed like a fly.

Marcus grunted. "I tried to do it, Declan, but I'm not to use my Will while in the palace."

For a man as strong in the power as Fenton, it was the work of a quick thought to seal a wound as trivial as the gash in my side. He wanted me kept tender.

"Noon, is it?" I asked. "You keeping me company until then?"

Fenton grinned and cracked his knuckles. "Seems like old times. Trouble in your road. I almost want you to run, just so I can smack you down."

I laughed, which felt better than grimacing. "Before this is through, you'll probably get your chance." I ran my tongue over my lips to get a taste of the lady in red. "The woman that stabbed me? She wore a red dress and a white mask— you always knew the comings and goings in this palace, Fenton, back in the day. I don't imagine that's changed. Who is she?"

A glimmer of uncertainty shimmered across his face. "I don't know." He was lying, I was sure of it. "We're investigating. An attack on the palace… should not have been possible." He cleared his throat. "But what do you expect, Hale? That your return would be met with wild jubilation? Word has spread throughout the city that you're here. Crowds have gathered in Elusive Square, and are clamoring for your head."

Marcus had brought some breakfast—bacon, eggs, and English muffins. After two failed attempts and a deep breath I finally sat up, then stood and limped over to the circular table near the window which overlooked the great city. Marcus helped me slip into a simple black polo shirt. I felt out of sorts without my waistcoat.

"No shoes?"

He shook his head. "I didn't have much in the way of currency, and I thought you'd appreciate something to eat more than something for your feet."

"Good call. Sophie?" I asked. Fenton and the two Knights joined us at the table as the smell of crispy meat wafted across the room.

"Fine. The kid, Ethan, convinced Clare to help him find Sophie. She was never in any danger—didn't even know there'd been some trouble at the shop. The Voidling was after you, and only you."

I nodded. "Good. Are they here?"

"Not Ethan and Sophie. Clare came back with her wounded unit. I told the other two to board up your shopfront and work on a few new wards."

"That's… optimistic."

Fenton chuckled. "So it's true? You opened a bookshop?"

"I thought it appropriately defiant." *And what has defiance got you so far?* "But tell me, Fenton. News has been thin on the ground in the real world. Tell me about Ascension City today. What's changed?"

"What's there to say? We are still rebuilding after you ended the war. We've held peace with the Renegades, for the most part. Both sides have factions, basically small scatterings of rebels who still don't see the fighting as over."

"How has Faraday kept peace with those bastards? King Renegade and his Immortal Queen would never accept anything less than—"

"Ah, that's where you're wrong." Fenton paused, then shrugged. "Well, you'll know soon enough anyway."

"What?"

"Faraday offered King Renegade an alliance. He took it. We're working with them now, Hale, to stop the spread of your Degradation and to undo the damage to the Story Thread. We're working together, both kingdoms as one, to find a way back into Atlantis."

Marcus scoffed. "That's not funny, Creed."

"I'm not joking."

"An… alliance?" I tasted the word on my tongue and found it bitter. "After all they've done, and that son of a bitch welcomes the Renegade dynasty *back* into Ascension City as if the last century of war never happened? Peace I can understand… but working *together*?"

"That's the gist of it, yes."

I could scarcely fathom such a decision. If I was reading the situation right, then my choices in Atlantis had not only ended the war, but forced the Knights and the Renegades, those that mattered, to turn from their own conflict and… Broken quill, the world was twice damned before lunch. "I'm going to eat the rest of the bacon."

Fenton agreed. "No sense being executed on an empty stomach."

~~*~*

"What of this merchant you were found with?" Fenton asked, as he escorted me to the washrooms. Marcus offered me his arm, which I gratefully accepted. My two guards kept pace just in our wake.

"Aaron? He's harmless. His only crime is having the misfortune to know me."

Marcus grumbled his agreement. "He's a good man. I spoke with him yesterday evening. Got a merchant's license to harvest in the Uncharted Realms after the war, and a nice little villa on the shores of Lake Delgado. He cooks and sells alchemical spices. His wife and son burned along with half of Ascension City after Declan unleashed the Degradation. Also works part-time as a custodian in the Forgetful Library. He's a good man, with no real love for this one." Marcus pointed at me.

Fenton seemed to take Marc at his word. "I'll see that he's released."

"Does my grandfather still work at the Library?" I asked. I'd not seen the old man in years. Aloysius Hale, my father's father. A tall, bespectacled gentleman unfortunate enough to share both a first and last name with two of Forget's most dangerous criminals.

"He was imprisoned for treason against the Dragon Throne," Fenton said.

"Ah, I thought something like that might have… no matter. He lives?"

"To my knowledge, yes. In relative comfort given his years of service as Chief Librarian. He wrote an interesting story after your banishment that proclaimed you as king, which was a harmless act in and of itself, until he littered the city with copies of the story. He also wrote that you prevented a Voidling invasion, through a reality storm, in the Thrice-Kindly works."

"He wrote all that? Well, it's mostly true, I guess."

"Stories upon stories," Marcus remarked, stroking his chin. "I don't like being back, but we've been away too long, Declan."

"I was just thinking the same thing."

"You should have stayed gone," Fenton said. "What happens next is your own doing."

"Oh, you never know. Maybe I'll be welcomed home with open arms."

CHAPTER FIFTEEN

We Three Kings

"I demand his head!" Morpheus Renegade growled. "My kingdom and realms will revolt if we allow Declan Hale, the Shadowless Arbiter himself, to go unpunished. His head, Faraday, or our alliance ends today."

"I will ask you to remember whose territory you currently reside in, King Renegade. It is my law here."

I had been brought before the entire court of the Knights Infernal and the ruling class of Ascension City. My arrival was big news, it seemed, and overnight envoys had been sent to the realms held by the Renegades—across the far-flung reaches of Forget. The lords of those lands had come themselves to ensure Faraday dealt with me.

I was happy to be wanted after being ignored for so long.

The ornate white chamber on the topmost floor of the Fae Palace, as vast as an ancient Roman pantheon, was cast in light from high arched windows amidst pristine pillars of marbled stone. *Fancy as shit.*

The Dragon Throne was made of black iron and set upon a crystal dais. Legend held that the throne was forged from the bones of an ancient dragon and sucked in the daylight like a possessed shadow. A part of me, and not a small part, heard the seat whispering my name.

I wasn't handcuffed, which was a small mercy, but Fenton waited nearby. At least a dozen more Knights stood guard behind him, not to mention the Knights forming a perimeter around the edge of the throne room and in the aisles between the rows of benches. If I so much as sneezed without permission...

Jon Faraday, his hands clasped behind his back, stood on the dais alongside Morpheus Renegade. Faraday was a young man—barely thirty—of average height, but solid. He wore a coat that hid cords of strong muscle. Morpheus was older, pushing sixty. His face was lined with wrinkles, craggy canyons, under a buzz cut of peppery-grey hair.

"I will ask you again, Hale," Faraday said. "What madness drove you back here? You were banished. To return covets death."

"Shall I be honest, Jon? I *missed* you," I said.

"The truth now." A thin crown, a simple golden band, rested on Faraday's shaven head. The circlet was inscribed with archaic runes, the indecipherable language of lost Atlantis.

"Because I have to be brave..." I muttered. "Because I never should have left."

"You should have died," Renegade said. He spoke as if his words should have been obvious to all assembled there. As if his truth was every truth. "How do you stand so arrogantly before us, casting no shadow as testament to your guilt? The weight of the crimes on your shoulders would crush any man with a heart."

"You're one to speak of hearts, Renegade. I'll see you dead one day, old man." I didn't care that I spat those words. "If I were still a Knight you would not be *welcome* in this palace."

"But you are not," Faraday said. He strolled to his stolen throne and sat. "And your return creates turmoil within peace. Your welcome was revoked. Your titles and honors stripped. It is because of you the Story Thread frays. This is not a time of war, yet I see no other judgment here today than… imprisonment in Starhold, and eventual execution."

"But he's such a sweet boy."

A soft voice, laced with hidden amusement, echoed across the vast hall. A thousand faces turned and beheld a woman in red wearing a porcelain facemask.

Amidst the mutterings of the assembled court, she strolled down the center aisle, between the rows of stone benches, and joined Renegade and Faraday on the dais overlooking the chamber.

Perplexed and wearing a mask of my own—one concealing a patient yet surly rage—I tilted my head and offered her a half-smile. Suddenly her true identity, and why she was here, came to me.

The Immortal Queen had entered the throne room.

"My lady," I said. "Why do you hide your face? I'm sure to look upon your beauty would pierce my heart like a knife to the side."

I couldn't be sure, but I felt her grin behind that mask. "Declan Hale is many things, but his actions allow both our kingdoms to flourish in peace after a century of dark war. It would be remiss to forget the good he has done. The end to our century of conflict and the lives that have been saved since."

I blinked. "Yeah, what she said."

The Immortal Queen stared at me from behind her mask. Her gaze was hot and unyielding. Being on the receiving end of that look was a most uncomfortable and intense sensation. Within those eyes, I could sense such a vast and lonely breadth of time, like the distant stars. Perhaps hers was more than just a title. Perhaps she really was immortal.

King Renegade slammed his gauntleted fists together. "What purpose does he serve alive? I tell you, none. You let him live, you let him *free*, and what manner of dark, Voidish mischief will he wreak against us next, my love?"

"He is an arbiter of change, for good or ill." The Immortal Queen stroked her husband's cheek. "But perhaps you are right, Morpheus. Declan Hale is too dangerous to run unchecked."

To my displeasure, I noticed Faraday seemed to actually consider those words. And here I was thinking I had more value alive than dead. Time to play my hand.

I cleared my throat. "Something is coming, fellas. And lady. Something… Voidish. I can feel it, creeping along my shadow. I dissuaded Voidlings from our realms once before, on the eve of the Degradation. When they try again you are going to need me."

"Give me a better reason," Faraday said. He rested his chin on his fist. "Well, Hale? You have more than earned execution. Breaking your exile alone was enough to ensure that. Half of Forget screams for your head, and the other half fears you. Those cries cannot go unheeded and your crimes cannot be pardoned. So what of it, Arbiter? Why will we need you?"

I gave the question more of my attention than it deserved. Once I'd dragged the moment out long enough, I stood up a little taller. "Well, I suppose I can unmake the Degradation, if you want."

For a brief moment, anyone there could have heard a pin drop from a mile away.

Then the room exploded into screams and chaos.

CHAPTER SIXTEEN

And Promises to Keep...

"Silence!" Jon Faraday, his voice amplified by Will, bellowed across the vast hall. The command echoed up into the vaulted ceiling and out over the wide balconies overlooking Ascension City far below.

After a moment, the hundreds of people assembled in the throne room regained some semblance of decorum. Soon the only sound was my soft, gentle laughter. Fenton and my guard seemed uncomfortable, and perhaps they sensed a sudden but inevitable betrayal. Good for them.

"Explain yourself, Declan," Faraday said with harsh intensity, which was good to hear. For the first time, I'd unnerved him.

I'd been watching Renegade and his queen during my shock announcement. Of her, I could read nothing behind that mask, but save for a slightly raised eyebrow, Morpheus hadn't seemed surprised. If anything, he looked satisfied. Perhaps I'd confirmed something he had already suspected.

"I can unmake the Degradation," I said. "There's a backdoor with a broken latch in the shield around Atlantis. I put it there, just in case." *Not entirely untrue.* "I came back because I can no longer bear to see the Story Thread unravel. It is time to undo past mistakes."

I was back to kill my murderer, whoever it may be, but only I knew that. What better way to draw them out than to dangle the greatest prize in all the worlds? Atlantis. Of course, if the future was to be believed then my actions, no matter what they were, led to a brutal death on the floor of my bookshop.

Knowing that was going to happen was perhaps enough warning to avoid it. Armed with a glimpse of the future I could change the past as I knew it. Such knowledge was what made the Historian so dangerous and respected. That made a strange kind of sense. I could only die trying.

"The Fourth and Fifth Legions battle alongside King Renegade's forces on the Plains of Perdition," Faraday said. "They surround the Degradation, Hale, but every day your blasted shield absorbs more of the Thread, widening and consuming Forget. Every day creatures, monsters or worse, emerge from within Atlantis and pass through the Degradation without harm. If it can be ended, then end it."

"Very well. I'll need access to the Plains of Perdition, and room to work. Send four bottles of your finest scotch to my room, and I'll get started."

Faraday shook his head. "I think not, given the attempt on your life last night." He glanced briefly at Renegade. "You will be imprisoned in Starhold until the path to Atlantis can be prepared. Our armies will scour the Plains and make it safe to work."

Starhold.

The Forgetful prison.

Ninety per cent of the inmates had good reason to hate me, more so than the people of Ascension City. I'd put them there, during my days as a Knight. Faraday had to know that. He had helped me, before everything went to shit. Cuffed in Will-suppression manacles, I'd be unlikely to survive an hour inside the celestial jail.

"If it's all the same to you, Jon, I'd rather not." *What game are you playing, you bastard?*

The good king allowed himself an uncharacteristic smile, which had very little warmth. "A few days in holding should make you more amenable to aiding the course of peace and justice, Hale. Take him away."

He waved his hand, and five Knights wearing full battle gear—armored chest plating and shielded facemasks concealing their identity—broke ranks with the rest and surrounded me. On each of their sleeves was the crest of Starhold—a six-pointed star above a spire of white stone—the Fae Palace.

These men were to be my jailers.

One of them produced a familiar pair of manacles and bound my wrists behind my back, good and tight. Bending my arms back pulled at the stitches in my side. If Emily could see me now... I missed her and her dancing. Seeing her smile a final time would have been worth the time to say goodbye.

Oh well.

I wanted to leave the throne room with a few scathing last words, but the fatigue enchantment was already making me drowsy. I yawned and winked at the Immortal Queen as I was dragged away and bundled into one of the elevators that hadn't been torn apart by hellish demons last night.

I left the Fae Palace the same way I'd arrived: under arrest, in handcuffs, and via the landing platform on the very summit of the obsidian crystal spire. Another two Starhold Knights, pilots from the look of them, awaited us in front of a fusion-powered cruiser. They accepted the prisoner transfer and stuffed me into the back of the paddy wagon. I was alone and fighting sleep. The cruiser was devoid of windows, and I sat in weak luminescent light as the thrum of the engines powered up and shook the small craft.

The cruiser took off above the city, no doubt on a flight path to the affluent western quarters and the launch complex capable of sending a ship to Starhold—a fitting name for the

Forgetful prison because it hung in orbit one hundred and fifty miles above Ascension City. Fighting the fatigue, I hadn't given up just yet, but escape was unlikely. *Escape into what? A city that hates you.*

Coming back had been a mistake, of course, but it was the only move I'd had left to make. Staying away, staying out, as Marcus had urged, was pure folly. Survival lay in action—not in a dusty bookshop, talking to story characters only I could see. Perhaps I was mad. The thought had occurred to me more than once.

I banged on the panel which separated my cage from the cockpit. "What say we swing by Mickey-D's and get some chicken nuggets?"

No response. With another yawn, I sat down and rested my head on my knees, trying to lessen the strain on my side from the tightly drawn cuffs. At some point, I must have drifted off to sleep, because I was suddenly jolted awake by the bump of the cruiser landing.

The door slid open on silent hydraulic hinges, and bright sunlight filled my holding cage. I squinted against the glare to allow my eyes to adjust, but I already knew something wasn't right.

We'd not arrived at the Starhold processing complex. We were not even in Ascension City. We had landed on the banks of Lake Delgado, thirty miles from the sprawling metropolis. Slick rifles in hand, my pilots stood dark and imposing against a backdrop of snow-capped mountains and a glittering, silver lake.

Two quick thoughts came to me: I was either being rescued or murdered, more likely the latter, given my current track record back here in Forget. One of the masked pilots stepped toward me and pulled the cover from his face.

From *her* face.

"You almost look surprised, Hale."

Clare Valentine produced a key and unlocked the star cuffs.

"What can I say?" I asked. "High treason against the crown suits you, sweet thing."

Clare took a deep breath and exhaled slowly. "You're too pretty for Starhold. They'll eat you alive up there."

Was Clare a part of Faraday's unseen plan? I honestly hoped not, but this escape seemed far too easy. Still, escape it was—and without any bloodshed.

Small mercies.

CHAPTER SEVENTEEN

Lonely Tonight

The other pilot removed his helmet and offered me a sly grin.

"Ethan?" Now I was surprised. "Oh, come on. Really?"

Ethan drew a pack of cigarettes from the pocket on his chest armor and lit up using a Willful thought. He took a long drag. "Hey, boss."

"What are you doing here?" No, poor question. "How did you... do any of this?"

"The kid here jumped at the chance to journey to Forget," Clare said.

"Half a week ago you knew nothing about this world. Now you're flying Starhold cruisers?"

He shrugged. "Miss Valentine did most of that. I just... wore the uniform."

"Come on, time for this later." Clare gazed up at the sky. "If they don't already know you're missing, they will soon. I disabled the tracking beacon in the wagon to buy us some time."

Clare set off at a steady pace along the shores of the lake, her boots crunching squeaky sand underfoot. Ethan stamped out his cigarette and took off after her. I followed at the rear, wincing as every step pulled at my stitches.

"I take it you have a plan?"

"A plan?" Clare asked, glancing over her shoulder. She stuck her tongue out at me. "No, I thought I'd make this up as I go along. You know, the Declan Hale special."

"There's a method to my madness."

"That remains to be seen."

"Sophie's here," Ethan said. "With the big fella and the... other big fella. Marcus and Aaron."

"I'm liking this more and more," I said. "Are we heading to his villa?"

Without looking back, Clare nodded. "Marc's waiting for us with a boat just around the bend in the shoreline up ahead. He'll take us across the lake."

Across the water, nestled between two mountains, was the town of Farvale. A mini-city, really, half-buried inside a pine forest. A long time ago, before I'd met Tal, Clare and I had snuck away from the Academy on a weekend and had gotten stupid drunk in that town. A lot of the recruits did—when we needed to get away from Ascension City and the Academy's brutal training regime.

How times change. Farvale was home to about twenty thousand people, if memory served. A good place to hide for a day or so, just on the outskirts in Aaron's home.

Marcus was waiting for us in an idling speedboat, a sleek silver craft with a sharp nose and matte finish. We splashed into the shallows and scurried aboard the vessel. The large man nodded at me once before gunning the throttle and launching the boat across the water. The boat ran swift and true as Marcus guided it along the outer rim of the lake.

Allowing myself a moment to rest properly, I held my head in one hand and my side with the other. No one spoke on the quick voyage. Marcus veered well to the right of Farvale. We passed other pleasure craft and tried to attract as little notice as possible. Something about the ease of my escape nagged at the back of my mind, but regardless, I expected to see those old familiar *Wanted* posters before too long.

Marcus shot straight for a small but homely-looking row of villas on the eastern shore of Delgado. He eased off on the throttle as we approached a private dock and came to a dead stop alongside the pier. Tying off the boat, we stepped ashore.

A majestic and proud hawk landed on my shoulder. The bird was mindful of its claws. "Chester," I said, greeting an old friend. "You been taking care of Aaron?" Clare and Ethan took off while I waited for Marcus to finish powering down the boat. Perhaps they sensed the same thing I did— that the giant man was pissed.

All seven feet of him hit the jetty hard and advanced on me.

Marcus grasped my arm and pulled me one staggering step to the side. Chester took flight with an indignant squawk.

"What do you think you're doing?" I asked.

"I warned you to stay away, to let it alone. And now look? It's you, Hale. It is always you. They follow you because you promise such... such *wonder*. You promise adventure in return for such cruel, bitter loyalty. And they end up dying for you!"

"I didn't ask you to pull me out of the fire, friend."

"I am not your friend. I've kept an eye on you during your exile, making sure you didn't do anything stupid... but here we are again. You are going to get Sophie *and* Ethan *and* Clare killed." He shook his head. "And what's worse is they don't see it. The poison you carry."

Trust Marcus, until he gives you a reason not to... A dead man had told me that, on the floor of my shop.

"We can't allow Morpheus Renegade—or Faraday—to seize what's in Atlantis. I don't know how, but I think they've figured out how to get at it." I rubbed at my stinging side. "It's why Tal and I did what we did, Marc. The Degradation. Why the better option was to let the Reach burn along with half of Ascension City. *Genocide* was better than letting anyone seize what we found in Atlantis."

"What could possibly be so important?"

A ghost of a smile flickered across my face. "The Infernal Clock."

~~*~*

Dusk fell over Lake Delgado, and from the balcony of Aaron's villa, I watched tiny fireflies dance across the surface of the water. I stood alone, contemplating the sordid past, the uncertain present, and the grim future.

"Are you coming in for something to eat?" Sophie asked. She stood just inside on the polished floorboards. Soft candlelight glowed behind her and cast flickering shadows across the living room.

The smell of spiced vegetables and fried meats wafted out into the open air. Aaron had always been an exceptional cook. "Did you come back to Forget for me or for Ethan, 'Phie?"

She shrugged and wrapped her arms around her abdomen against the cool breeze. "I'm just glad to be back. Everything here is just so much *more*, Declan. The air is sweeter, the water fresher. You know, like…"

"Like a fairytale, yeah." I moved slowly but surely over the threshold and back inside, putting an arm across Sophie's shoulders. The wound in my side was paining me something awful. "I even got stabbed by a wicked witch."

"Yeah I heard. Do you want me to try and heal it?"

"Could you?" I raised an eyebrow. "I mean, I didn't think you were that far along skill-wise."

"Unlike you, I've not spent the last five years drinking away what little talent I have. Here." She lifted my shirt, exposing the ugly crescent-shaped cut in my side and Fenton's crude crisscrossing stitches. "Yes, I can heal that."

"Okay, please don't set fire to my kidneys…"

Sophie pooled smoky luminescent light into her palm and pressed it against my red-raw skin. Her touch tingled, and a tiny furrow appeared in her brow as she concentrated on the enchantment. After a moment, I felt the skin ripple and the stitches melt away.

She removed her hand. "Doesn't that look pretty now."

"Barely a scar. Thanks, 'Phie. Still hurts a bit, though. Help me sit down?"

Sophie helped me to a seat on the leather sofa next to the fireplace. Chester flew from his perch and settled on my knee. His golden eyes stared unblinking into mine. I stroked the feathers about his neck.

The chef had out done himself. Plates of sizzling meat and warm breads were arrayed across the coffee table. Marcus, Ethan, Clare, and Aaron had already helped themselves and were chatting quietly in between bites of the delectable food. The heady aromas of sharp spices were damn near dizzying.

"What are you staring at, Declan?" Clare asked.

I blinked and fell out of my swirling thoughts. I'd been staring at nothing but the far wall. "Is that a liquor cabinet? How did that slip by me?"

Chester flapped over onto Sophie's knee as I stood up. I cast a quick look at Aaron, and he smirked. Sure enough, the cabinet was locked. Without really thinking about it, I snapped my fingers, and the door clicked open. Inside I found renewed hope that everything would be okay.

"Macallan's Single Malt Scotch Whisky… *eighty years old*." I cradled the bottle to my chest, wiping some of the dust away. "Ladies and gentlemen, a toast!"

"I'm surprised it took you this long," Aaron remarked. "Just a drop, I suppose."

The cabinet held a set of crystal whisky glasses, and I placed them out on the coffee table between the two sofas. "None for you, Chester. You're flying in the morning." As for the rest of us, the consequences could go hang themselves.

"Isn't he a little young for this stuff?" Clare asked me as I handed Ethan a glass of amber liquid.

"Oh, sure. Too young for scotch but old enough to break a condemned man out of prison. Young enough to die, Clare." I knew that better than most. "Come on, we've got to acknowledge the commitment we've made today—to ourselves, to Atlantis and all its many splendored wonders."

Marcus shrugged and accepted a glass. Clare looked as though she had something more to say, but decided against it. Maybe she really was on my side and a thorn in Faraday's. Or maybe sponsoring a little underage drinking was nothing compared to our other crimes.

"What commitment?" Ethan asked.

"To saving the world, rookie."

"I didn't realize it was in peril," Sophie said.

"Given what's at stake, we're probably the only people in all Forget who can stop what's about to happen."

"And what is about to happen?" Aaron popped a red date into his mouth.

"I don't know what game Faraday or Renegade are playing, but I do know we can't let either of them take Atlantis. I told them I could end the Degradation, and Renegade acted as if that didn't matter. I think he may have found a way through the shield without me."

"Is that possible?" Marcus asked, then sipped at his drink.

I thought of the Immortal Queen and the dagger she had used to stab me. What had she done with that dagger? Or more specifically, the blood on it? Having my blood may have made it possible to breach the city.

"There's magic in what we are," I said, holding my glass before me against the flames of the fire. Looking a touch confused, my compatriots joined me. Five shadows danced on the rich mahogany walls, all save mine. "We are real magic, folks. None of the flashing lights and broken Will stuff we do every damn day. What we are is very rare."

We were the fire against the indifference to the threat of Faraday, of Renegade and his damned armies. We were not a force of *good*; we were a force of *necessity*. I'd ended a war once, out of necessity. I shook my head and thought of what to say next—something meaningful that would inspire courage in my few precious companions. I came up with nothing, and suddenly, the very idea seemed absurd.

"Here's to magic," I said, raising my glass and finally embracing the word. I paused, then tossed the scotch back with a practiced flick, and relished the burn down the back of my throat. The others took small sips, perhaps savoring the taste.

"May it make sense with time," Aaron added, inclining his glass toward me. He looked old, done in. "It will get better with time…"

I had to remind myself that Atlantis was still a myth to my friends. Inaccessible and lost. But I had been there. Tal had been there.

"No," I said. "No, no. Just liquor. Time's no good, old friend."

Time was a bitch.

Time was a headache and a slow, painful death on a shop floor.

But then time wounds all heels, doesn't it, Declan? And in the end it would settle all of our accounts with merciless efficiency. There was a dark, certain thought in a world where nothing was certain save uncertainty. Was I really that miserable?

Maybe I was just insane—the lesser of two certainties and a thought that just wouldn't quit. Oh well.

"Wonder what else they have on tap here…" I muttered, and turned back to the liquor cabinet.

CHAPTER EIGHTEEN

Master Bolt

Clare was awake and making coffee when I stumbled into Aaron's kitchen the next morning. I had a most regretful hangover. She looked great in the early light with her disheveled crimson red and electric blue hair. She wasn't wearing her Knightly garb, just a shirt, shorts, and a pair of baggy knee socks.

"You look odd without a waistcoat," she said as I limped over to the fridge.

I straightened my collar and smirked. "If I don't look the part, then how am I supposed to act the part, is that it?" I found eggs, some Italian bread, bacon, leftover chicken breast, tomatoes... I had an idea. Was there garlic? Ah, a single clove.

"The part?" Clare spooned a healthy tablespoon of sugar into her coffee and sat stirring it idly as she stared at me from behind her multi-colored fringe.

I deposited my ingredients on the marble countertop and sorted the meat from the greens from the bread rolls. "Never mind. I'm not much of a cook, sweet thing, but I can make one helluva filling sandwich. You hungry?" She shrugged. "Sure you are. Want to give me a hand? Poach some eggs while I chop tomatoes?"

Clare smiled—another one of those uncertain certainties this early in the game. "You know, despite the danger, Declan, I'm glad you're not cooped up in that bookshop. It's a dreary place."

And I think it drove me mad. Madder. "Me too, actually. I'd grown far too accustomed to the silence."

"And the writing."

"I enjoy the writing."

Clare helped me make breakfast. Ascension herbs on the bread rolls added a touch of local flavor to the whole ordeal. I wrapped the chicken breasts in crispy bacon, and then I sliced tomato, diced onion, scooped relish sauce, and topped it all off with a poached egg. There was no mayonnaise, unfortunately, but the smell of good honest food wafting through the villa brought the others to join us before it could all get cold.

We had sandwiches for breakfast, and they were good.

Afterwards, I laid out the plan for reaching Atlantis. I only glanced over the Degradation, as I was not quite willing to discuss what needed to be done there. The Degradation would be a bridge to burn when we reached the damn thing. Getting to the Lost City would be hard enough, if not damn near impossible. Someone, perhaps everyone, would most likely die for this folly.

Yet it had to be done, and I'd go alone if all else failed, for the right reasons as well as the selfish ones. I couldn't let Morpheus Renegade or his queen seize the city, not with the secret buried in its heart. Whoever took the Infernal Clock, took Forget. The Knights would fall under an unstoppable Renegade onslaught.

In the early morning light, Aaron's balcony overlooking Lake Delgado didn't seem a grim enough venue for the topic of our conversation, but it would have to do.

"So the Degradation ties Atlantis to our reality, Declan?" Aaron asked. "A way between the worlds?"

"As best as I can explain it, yeah." Not like the book diving, or the portals that skimmed the Void. As our toast last night had promised, this was old magic. Real magic. Gone-too-far magic. "After stumbling across *Tales of Atlantis* all those years ago, Tal and I used it to forge a path into the city. We were young and stupid, and had no idea what was sleeping there."

"But why? I mean, what's so terrible about Atlantis? What could Faraday, or Morpheus Renegade do, if they won the city?" Aaron rested his hands on his not inconsiderable gut. He seemed genuinely perplexed.

I grinned, wishing I had another breakfast sandwich. "Do? Oh, not much. Just unleash the demonic forces of Hell that destroyed the Old World and pushed humanity back ten thousand years. Basically send us right on over the brink of extinction. Atlantis died all that time ago for a *very* good reason."

Aaron paled. He heard the dread conviction in my voice. "Oh."

"Yeah. Ascension City had just a taste five years ago, before I used the Degradation to seal Atlantis again." I slapped the old merchant on the back. "But not to fret, eh? We've got about a day before we need to worry about that. That's our job, mate. Beat the bastards there, gain access to the city, undo the Degradation and take away any reason for being there. After that, well, time... *time*, is different in Atlantis. Stretched..."

"What do you mean?" Sophie asked, her eyes wide and fascinated.

I looked at Tal's sister and wished things were different for her. She was very young and very pretty. I should send her home, really, and save her the pain... but something made me hesitate. Some instinct, a gut feeling sent by Oblivion itself, no doubt.

"That's what happened. What we did, Tal and I. *Why* we did it. We forced a tear into the Void, and dared King Renegade to seize the city. To put an end to the Tome Wars and at the same time seal away the monstrosities running rampant over Ascension City. We couldn't have known what was housed in Atlantis. In its heart. Do you understand? We couldn't have known."

"What? What was there?" Clare licked her lips and paused. "Declan, let's have the truth now."

"The Infernal Clock, among other things. There's another fairytale made real for you."

Ethan took the bait, even as Marcus sighed and covered his face with his hands. "Other things?"

Sophie began to weep. She knew this part. I'd owed her this much for killing her sister.

"One of the Everlasting," I said.

A shadow seemed to fall across the room, and it couldn't have been mine.

"The Everlasting?" Ethan asked into the silence.

"If you'd had a proper education, in the Academy, you would know their names. Every Knight knows their names. Oblivion, Scion, Chronos... There are nine of them." *For mortal men doomed to die...* "For all that matters, they are gods. Old gods. Until Atlantis, until Tal and I, no human being had ever dealt with them face to face, as far as we knew. They were a story, the first story, handed down across aeons. *Just* a story."

"And you met one?"

"'Met' is too kind of a word, but yes, I did. Tal was with me. Only for a handful of minutes, but when we were done my shadow had been torn away, Tal's essence was scattered across all the realms of existence, and the Degradation encased Atlantis like a death shroud."

Hopeless quiet greeted my words. Only Marcus and Sophie had known about my encounter with something from beyond... *everything*—the Earth, the Forgetful realms, the Void. The Everlasting belonged to none of them. Not to the universe or the space between universes. It terrified me.

"How do you intend to unmake the Degradation?" Aaron asked. "The best scholars and most powerful men and women in Forget haven't been able to even dent that monstrosity in five long years."

"Simple, really. We kill its fuel supply. Choke it and watch it die."

"Again, I must ask. How?"

The "how" was the crux of the matter. The truth within the lie I'd told the ruling class before the Dragon Throne yesterday morning, just before I was sentenced to space prison. "I've already mentioned the Infernal Clock, but what do you know of it?"

"It's supposed to grant eternal life," Clare said. "Immortality."

I nodded. "I saw it once. I was almost close enough to touch it when the Everlasting made Tal and I barter for the Degradation. Our own fault, I suppose. We stumbled into Its lair and woke the darn thing up."

"Which one was it?" Marcus asked. "It was Oblivion, wasn't it? You dealt with Lord Oblivion in front of the Infernal Clock. Just like the old fairytale goes." He shook his head, unable to believe what he was saying.

"It was Oblivion, yes. He… It… offered us a deal. It tricked us, but we got what we wanted, in the end. Atlantis was sealed away, and Renegade's army was scattered across the Plains of Perdition as the Degradation came into being." I thought back to the terrible day. An endless night upon an endless prairie. "The Infernal Clock is the master bolt in the shield's design. It's not actually a clock, like with hands and a face. But it does keep time, and if we sever the Clock, the whole darn shield comes crashing down."

Marcus cursed. "So your solution to the Degradation is to cut out the very heart of the Story Thread? Declan, wasn't one apocalypse enough for you?"

"Think of it more like a diseased limb that needs amputating. Tal and I used the Infernal Clock as a linchpin of power, to fuel the Degradation. If it can be removed…"

"Madness. End-of-the-world-type madness."

"Perhaps, but there's a taste of redemption in it, don't you think?"

"And without the Clock, Atlantis is just a ruined husk of a city, yes?" Aaron stood and clapped his hands together. "No reason to fight over it. No reason for war. Well, what do you know? A cord of rationale buried within Declan's lunacy after all."

~~*~*

Later that afternoon, as the sun crowned the peaks of the western mountains, I sat in the living room next to the liquor cabinet, and scrawled on loose-leafed parchment with a fountain pen. Sophie found me there and sat down quietly on the rug to watch me write.

"Sophie, there you are. Where've you been hiding? I just sent Ethan off to find you in the gardens."

Sophie's smile was strange, confident. She looked happy. "I've been at the markets in Farvale with Aaron all morning. Have you seen the town? It's wonderful. I ate a honeysuckle dragonfly!"

"Gross."

"Delicious. And look…" She glanced about and then leaned in close, pulling her shirt aside and revealing her left breast. There was a silver bar running through her nipple. "They didn't even ask for ID. I'd forgotten what this place was like. Think Ethan will like it? I love being home, Declan."

I grasped at my own nipple and winced. "Ouch. Why?" I shook my head. "No, never mind. You're right about being home. Despite the prison sentence and impending doom, this is where we belong, 'Phie. But, you know, if you and Ethan want to leave now and avoid the fight to come…"

Sophie poked her tongue out at me, then pressed the soles of her shoes together and rocked side to side. "Really? I stuck with you for five years, Declan. You know why. I'm not about to change teams now."

"It's not about changing teams. More like stepping off the field and living your life without my troubles hanging over you like the sword of fucking Damocles."

"From what you've said, Forget may not be worth living in much longer if the Knights or the Renegades manage to take Atlantis. So I'll fight for that, if you don't mind—or even if you do." Sophie stood up. "Right, Ethan's in the gardens. Where's Marcus hiding?"

I straightened up the pages, blowing on the ink to help it dry. "I sent him back to Perth, to the shop. There's a book we need to cross over into the Plains of Perdition. A scary, scary book."

"He's due back soon?"

"Before sunset, if we're lucky. Later on tonight if we're not. At dawn tomorrow we make the trip and see about averting catastrophe."

Sophie headed outside in search of Ethan, and I threw my latest pages into the hot coals which simmered in the fireplace. The writing had only been a distraction from the waiting. If I wanted I could go wandering around Farvale, but with a face as recognizable as mine, wandering was probably a bad idea.

With a sigh, I rubbed at my eyes and licked my lips. I wanted something fizzy, for a change, such as a can of Coke or something. The Forget may have held every territory ever written by the Willful, but the bulk of True Earth's delicacies often found their way over, one way or another—particularly in and around Ascension City, where the majority of humanity crossed between the realms.

I made my way toward the kitchen. My bare feet were silent against the wooden floorboards, which is why I heard the two gentle voices before I saw them. I slowed to a stop just in the hall outside of the kitchen and eavesdropped.

"Trust me when I say this," Aaron said. "You do not want Declan Hale fighting this war again. He is ruthless."

"That's good for a war, isn't it?" Ethan asked, obviously not in the gardens. I heard the fridge open and close, the rustle of brown paper bags. They were putting away the supplies purchased in Farvale.

Aaron sighed. "Spoken by a man who has never fought in one. You misunderstand, because you cannot understand. Declan is kind, caring, and loyal. He is all of these things, yet he is ruthless. In war he is driven by rage. In the final years of the last conflict, he committed such atrocities. The Degradation was almost among the least of them."

"What did he do?"

"What was necessary to protect what he believed. In *whom* he believed."

"That doesn't sound so bad," Ethan remarked.

"No?" Aaron chuckled without humor. "Again, you cannot understand. I took lives in the war, young Ethan. Many lives. Some deserved death, and some did not. But *I* never wielded true power. Not like Declan. In the final days of the war, just before he created the Degradation, the penultimate battle was fought in a realm of Forget known as the Reach. A city of millions... Declan used a weapon he found in Atlantis during his Great Quest to fight in that battle." Aaron sighed.

"What weapon?"

"A sword. A terrible sword capable of harnessing an absurd amount of Will. He lost control, Reach City burned, and Declan's little secret was exposed. With Atlantis at risk, he chose to seal away the city... at the expense of the Story Thread."

"And now that's he going back? What will happen?"

"I wish I knew. He's changed. Perhaps for the better, perhaps not. Only the guilty can understand the cost of true power, Ethan. And Declan is very guilty. Millions of innocents suffered and died for his ambition. Let us hope he has learned from that mistake. Yet I can't help but feel the last five years were nothing more than a brief interlude between conflicts." Aaron sniffed. "Last time, Declan had Tal Levy—Sophie's sister—to fight for. Now he does not. Now he has... just his anger. I'm terrified we're helping a madman gain inconceivable power."

"You could... talk to him about this."

"And say what? No, we must watch. We must help him *avoid* the war." One of them turned on the sink tap. "Besides, I am not nearly brave enough to anger Declan Hale. No, no, no."

I'd heard enough. Aaron's words did ignite a spark of frustration in my heart, but I liked to think I'd changed since the end of the Tome Wars, since my choices had forced Tal's death. Fair to say I'd paid a handsome price for my *ruthlessness*. Stepping away from the kitchen, I headed out to the balcony once more for some fresh air. My ire had to be directed towards my true enemies.

Jon Faraday.

Morpheus Renegade. His stab-happy wife.

And anyone else that gets in your way, Dec? whispered a voice in the back of my head.

How far would Faraday go? His acceptance of Renegade into the Fae Palace had been a surprise, but he wasn't stupid enough to actually trust the snake. Not in a million years. The heat death of the universe would pass us by before Faraday would so much as blink in Renegade's presence. So what was the plan? The end game? Plunge both kingdoms back into war? Too simple.

The sun disappeared behind the mountains, casting violet halos on the craggy peaks.

The solution came back to Atlantis, and what could be won there. The fate of the new world order would be decided in the ruins of the old.

CHAPTER NINETEEN

I Ain't Happy

I went into the kitchen for that Coke I'd been craving earlier. With the rest of the gang missing, the villa was a quiet place. I knew Clare had been upstairs earlier, so I set off to find her, two fizzy drinks in hand.

Dusk light filtered in through the skylight in the hallway upstairs. "Clare?"

"In here, Declan."

I followed her voice down the hall and into the bedroom she and Sophie had shared last night. The door was ajar, and the subtle scent of cinnamon drew me in and left me wanting to sit down and sigh. I was a long way past regret for what could have been in my life. Still, I couldn't help but want at these simple moments of perdition.

Clare was seated in a window bay that overlooked the magnificent lake and mountains. The failing light caught her lounging in a silk blouse and shorts. A golden aura of energy seemed to cling to her form, to follow the curves from her bare feet up to her avian-like face.

My heart skipped a few beats. I felt a familiar surge of longing—of raw desire. She wasn't just gorgeous. She was *beautiful* and made me feel my age, for once. Young before war's end, before Tal.

"You're staring, Declan."

"Sorry. Breathtaking view up here, is all."

Clare smiled at the not-so-subtle compliment. She accepted the Coke with a word of thanks and twisted off the screw cap to release that satisfying *hiss* of bubbles. "The first sip is always the best."

"I was lonely, so I came looking for a friend."

"Oh, we're friends, are we?" Clare took her first sip. "Not just old lovers who hook up once every half-decade? Or break one another out of custody? Risk treason and execution? I don't know what we are, Declan, but I am confused."

I sat on the edge of the window niche and gently stroked Clare's ankle. "I know, and although the words are too small to convey any true meaning, I *am* sorry for all the trouble. I know I can be... ruthless, sometimes."

Clare rolled her eyes. "You've just never gotten over the girl you couldn't have. Tal was lovely, Declan. She was kind and lovely. But she's gone. Long gone. Move on, would you?"

Everything was tied to Tal, wasn't it? My every choice, every victory, and every defeat came back to her. Love was a many splendored thing.

"Is it that simple?" I asked. Never mind the armies of Forget were on the move. Never mind I had just over a day left to live, if the past was to be believed... "I loved her, Clare. I still *love* her. So very much."

"And that's fine, very human even. I'd be worried if you felt any other way. I know losing Tal—never really having her—makes you feel torn open inside. Declan, that's a good thing. That's a goddamn strength. You'd be broken and finished if you didn't feel that bad from losing someone you love. But she is gone, and you're wanting after something you can't have. Typical man."

"I did have her once. On the eve of the Degradation in the ruins of Nightmare's Reach. I told her I loved her and she said… heh… she smiled and said thank you."

Clare closed her book, a finger between the pages, and crossed her legs. "I never knew that."

I shook my head. "No one did. She died later that night. That endless night."

"I'm sorry, Declan, for your loss. I don't know if anyone has ever said that. I guess if no one knew…"

"Sophie knew I loved her. That's why she stuck with me through the exile." I sighed a sigh for the ages. "Thanks, Clare."

"Honestly though, you can't have her. So move on."

"Easier said than done, sweet thing. I… I try not to think about it. Sometimes I get so absorbed in my writing—or a bottle of scotch—that I go an entire half a day without thinking of her. Sometimes. But…"

"But?"

"I let myself think of nothing but her—for five minutes at the end of the day. Five minutes where I let myself *bask* in the regret of what happened. The one I lost, who I never really had. It's futile, I know. Five ultimately pointless minutes that do nothing but hurt, yet I reckon I'll be doing it right up until the day I die."

So, just once more then, according to the Historian. Grand.

"Well, this is just a whole other side of you. You're always closed off. Emotionally flat. I think you're actually feeling so much so often that you're broken."

Emily Grace had said something similar, under the hot lights and amidst the fierce music at Paddy's only a few short nights ago. *I think you're trying very hard not to cry.* I missed her.

"You kissed me," I said, changing the subject rather abruptly.

"Yes. And you kissed me back."

"May I kiss you again?"

Clare leaned in so close that our noses almost touched. "No," she said, her breath warm against my face. Then she pressed her lips against mine softly, just for a heartbeat.

I laughed, enjoying her secret smile and affection. "Please do that again…"

Clare uncrossed her legs and returned to her book. "You need to think about what it is you want, Declan. Goodnight."

~~*~*

"Did you get all of it?" I asked.

Marcus made it back to the villa early the next morning, as most of us were sitting around the kitchen. Something as simple as cornflakes should've taken the magnificence out of breakfast in Forget, but if anything, the mundane cereal only enhanced the view of the forest-city further down the lake and added a sense of reality to the unreality.

Sugar to the spice.

"I brought you some clothes and shoes," he said, stomping through the kitchen unshaven and tired.

A knot of dread settled in my stomach at the sight of the backpack slung over Marcus's enormous shoulder. I already knew what was in there. I *knew* it.

He unzipped the bag and tossed me a white collared shirt and a pair of trousers—all wrapped up in my favorite grey waistcoat.

I can't save you from that wound, I'd told my dying self. *All the Will in the world couldn't… Are you wearing my favorite grey waistcoat?*

My funeral suit. Oh… goody. I pushed away the bowl of cornflakes. Suddenly, I wasn't so hungry anymore. Still, the clothes were better than the dirty polo shirt and jeans I'd been wearing for two days.

"And then there's this," Marcus said, and handed me a book in a brown paper bag. "Really, you just left it sitting on the counter?"

"Hidden in plain sight."

"What is it?" Clare asked, running her spoon through the milky dregs of her breakfast.

"*Tales of Atlantis.* How Tal and I found the Lost City, back in the day."

"Hmm. Go get changed, would you?" Clare stopped running her foot up and down my leg under the table. "You don't look like you without the vest."

"You'll be the death of me, sweet thing."

I excused myself and headed upstairs to the shower. Better to die well dressed, I suppose, although I was still a few pieces short of solving that grim puzzle. The man who had died on my shop floor had had a fresh scar cutting down his face and a gaping wound in his gut. Knowing it was coming, perhaps it could still be avoided.

Sophie and Ethan were cuddled up together on the leather sofa in the living room, sketching crude drawings of the mountains over the far side of the lake, when I came downstairs. Ascension City was just on the other side of those peaks.

Sophie laughed as Ethan stroked the small of her neck, just behind her ear.

Kids.

"Good morning, you two."

"Hey, Mr. Hale," Ethan said.

I offered him half a smile. "Call me Declan, Reilly. You've earned it."

Sophie rolled her eyes. "You need a shave."

I rubbed at my stubbly cheeks. "So, here's the thing. You two are heading back to Perth this morning. I'm sending you on a super-secret important mission to, uh, go have fun at the beach or something."

Sophie glared. "What?"

"Just until all this plays out, one way or another." I held out my hands and, after a moment, Sophie and Ethan each gave me one of their own. "This isn't your fight, even if you want it to be. Neither of you are ready for this. Sophie, you were just a kid during the last war, and Ethan—despite your daring rescue—this is your first time in Forget. You're untrained and worse, eager to please."

"That's not really fair, is it?" he said, pulling back his hand.

Sophie shrugged. "I'll stay if I want, Declan." She glanced at her boyfriend. "But I don't think I want to, not really."

"'Phie?"

"Hush, Ethan. Declan's right, in his own idiotic way. We've no reason to be here, and we'll most likely get in his way."

"But if we stay, then I won't have to do uni exams next week."

I snorted. "Well, at least you've got your priorities straight."

After a long moment in silence, I let go of Sophie's hand and sighed.

"You're not leaving, are you?"

"Not a chance," she said. "Not with what's at stake."

Kids.

~~*~*

So, just the six of us to save the big, cruel world and all of Forget.

Or at least stop the whole mess from slipping any closer to oblivion.

"Anyone want to back out, now's your chance. We're going about as deep into Forget as you can go. To the very edge of the Degradation."

"This isn't going to end well," Marcus said. "For any of us."

Trust Marcus… until he gives you a reason not to.

"Chin up, sailor."

Tales of Atlantis sat on the coffee table. We circled around the table and the book of short stories, written a long time ago by the last people to see Atlantis before it fell into the seas of chaos.

"It's either you or Clare who'll have to do the diving invocation," Marcus said. "Sophie, Ethan, and I are tied to True Earth, not to Ascension City."

That was true. Using a book as a gateway, diving through the pages, meant remaining tied to the point of origin—True Earth for Sophie, Ethan, and Marcus, which meant they couldn't dive again unaided. To sever their tether would be to risk falling into the Void, slipping sideways out of existence.

Just one of the many rules of diving across universes. You could only go one level deep. Earth to Forget. Clare had come the other way, Forget to Earth. She was tied to Ascension City, and I had crossed the Void through the Black Mirror, which had been forged here.

Sophie, Marcus, Ethan—and Aaron, who possessed not one drop of Will—would have to ride alongside either Clare or myself.

Ethan spun the book around on the table. "So if Atlantis was lost for so long, how come this book can get you there?"

"It gets you close," I said, "to the plains the city was built upon all those millenniums ago, and the Degradation. It's hard to explain, but Atlantis used to be a part of Earth—of True Earth, where all of us save Aaron were born. Atlantis fractured, Ethan. Some travesty in the past forced the city into Forget."

"There are theoreticians at the Academy in the Fae Palace that believe Atlantis was, perhaps, the very *first* piece of Forget," Aaron said and stroked his chin. "The first realm to form and claim the nothing-space the Void occupied. From Atlantis, all the rest of Forget formed, like an archipelago. What we call the Story Thread. Not just worlds upon worlds tied together, but universes upon universes."

"And you just happened to have a copy of this book lying around?" Clare asked, glaring at the damn thing. "Broken quill, if Faraday knew..."

"I found it not even a week ago, on the shores of Diablo Beach back in Perth." I grunted. "Which tells us one thing. Someone, perhaps even Faraday himself, wanted me back in Forget. To try for Atlantis."

A silence fell over the group, and I felt cold, though the day outside was warm and bright.

"We're diving into a trap," Sophie said. "But there's no other way, is there?"

"Not to where we're going. So let's get it over with." I rolled up my sleeves and picked up *Tales of Atlantis*. "Clare, grasp the cover. The rest of you, hold on tight to either of our arms. This will be a bumpy ride."

Aaron shifted his duffel bag from one shoulder to the other. "I've only ever done this once before," he said.

"It's like riding a bike... across a thin wire over a nightmarish chasm of horror," I assured him.

"Chin up, sailor?" Marcus asked.

I let the Will flow down my arms and into the thin book of old stories. "Something like that."

We slipped along the ragged edge of the burning page... and straight into a warzone.

SILENCE THE GUNS: PART III

Wastelands aside, he cannot win.
Those soulless eyes, that bloody grin.
No sword or defiance will scar,
His broken will—a distant star.

~The Historian of Future Prospect
After Madness, 2007

You were unsure which pain was worse—the shock of
what happened or the ache for what never will.

~Simon Van Booy

Perhaps a secret—
Or pencil in hand,
Enriched the pure leaf
Made true, after all
Scorn the fool's last piece.

~King Morrow's Journal (Vol. VII)

CHAPTER TWENTY

The Perdition War

The Tome Wars had been a time of anarchy and rampant destruction. When people capable of harnessing the powers of creation used that power to make war, the result was always catastrophic. Before my fall, I'd been a hero, in the cruelest sense of the word.

I'd used my strength to shatter entire legions of Renegade's soldiers.

I'd foiled plots and assassination attempts against King Morrow—Faraday's predecessor.

I'd won battles that were hopeless, waged crusades in the face of insurmountable defeat and snatched victory from the jaws of Oblivion. I became a figurehead for the war effort, and as a Knight—a lord of Ascension City—I was groomed for the throne.

The penultimate battle in Reach City, which had ended the lives of so many, so suddenly, had changed all that. My hand had been forced at the cruel point of the Roseblade. I'd used the epic sword to change all Forget. Atlantis was no longer a secret anymore. The myth had been dragged screaming into the light. I'd long since attracted Morpheus Renegade's attention, his ire, but that night he turned his whole might against me—the war was no longer Knights against Renegades.

It was Knights and Renegades against Declan Hale.

And I'd won, damn it, at a cost so great that there were too many dead to bury.

When the war came down to that last, awful night, the choice had been either Reach City or the very linchpin that held Forget together. I'd chosen to save Forget, for the greater good. *And for her...* One day I might even come to terms with that.

My companions and I came spinning out of the Void under a hail of Will fire and clouds of thick, choking smoke.

The Plains of Perdition were ablaze with war.

Tales of Atlantis had spat us out on the edge of a vast field cradled between two valleys that reached a single point in the distance. That point intersected with a monumental purple dome of light, atop a long grassy ridge.

The Degradation.

Arcs of multi-colored light, sizzling beams of energy designed to kill, cut through the air. A large battle was being waged before the Degradation, upon the Plains. At a quick glance, I saw the heavy cloaks of the Knights clashing against the darker uniforms of a Renegade army. The conflict was sweeping toward us and burning large swaths of the valley in its wake.

"Looks like Faraday's precious alliance is over," I said, pooling Will into my palms and readying both offensive and defensive enchantments. "Look at all those poor bastards."

"This is..." Ethan's eyes bulged. "This is insane! Is that a *dragon*?"

"Sure is, chief." I slapped him on the back with my glowing hand. "Welcome to paradise."

The thing about Will, and the realms we traversed using Will, was that damn near anything and everything could be brought from one world to the next. Creatures, such as dragons, could be transported across realms. The black market trade on such exotic animals had flourished during the Tome Wars, which was half the reason why the war had been so devastating and why the Knights had done all they could to protect Ascension City and True Earth from the Renegades.

A war of Will fought along the Story Thread could only end in madness.

Men and women, clad in bloody armor, fought in no discernable formations. Narrow beams of fire and hot lightning rocketed back and forth through the air while shields of Will flared to life and deflected or dispersed most of the attacks. The beams they missed engulfed Knights and Renegades alike.

I saw a velociraptor tear out a man's throat.

A band of tiny creatures, that resembled a group of leprechauns, flew through the air and left trails of golden sparks in its wake along the edge of the battle. Each spark liquefied armor and flesh.

Ethan's dragon breathed jets of flame across a unit of Knights. They emerged unscathed under an emerald shield of Will.

Something that looked as if it belonged to Lovecraft's mad Arab pulled its enormous weight across the ground, all tentacles and porous skin, leaving a deep furrow in its wake full of bubbling acid.

Clare was at my side. "They're slaughtering each other."

"What else is new?" I sighed. "We have to reach the shell of the Degradation—if we're not already too late. The Queen's had my blood for days. She and her blasted husband already may have used it to get through. Come on."

The group set off at a jog, Aaron huffing and puffing at the rear, along the outskirts of the battle.

"We'll take a half day to even reach the shell if we stick to the edges," Marcus observed. "This is foolish, Declan."

"I'm open to suggestions here."

"We—"

A ten-foot lance of white ice struck the ground in front of us and exploded in a thousand deadly shards. I reacted almost instantly, as fast as thought. A wall of superheated flame burst to life between my group and the ice, melting the deadly projectiles as they flew through the wall and soaked us in a harmless spray of warm water.

The battle had turned.

Trouble in our road.

Hordes of travesties and war-raged soldiers threatened to overwhelm us. Clare, Marcus, and myself—the most experienced, the veterans—kept up a steady flux of mostly defensive Will work. A cacophony of charmed light doused flames, absorbed lightning, and melted steel.

We were good. The best, once upon a time—at the start of all the great stories, yes, yes—but there was only so much we could do against the immense tide of warring Knights and Renegades.

A wave of concussive force from behind sent us all reeling head over heels across the ground. The group was split, and the tide washed in, separating Clare and me from the others.

I watched as Marcus deflected a Renegade soldier's fiery sword blow to save Ethan's life. Sophie snarled and sent a bolt of sizzling energy into the man's chest plate—frying his insides. Her snarl turned into a surprised gape as she realized what she'd done.

"Marc, Aaron!"

Marcus glared at me over the heads of the soldiers between us and swung around to find Aaron, who was being attacked by a spider grown to about the size of a Mini Cooper.

Aaron swung his duffel bag of supplies in the creature's face, and its long, gore-spattered fangs sunk into the material and tore it apart. The contents of the bag sprayed across the field.

"No!" Aaron yelled, and dived beneath the giant spider.

The battle intensified, and the last glimpse I had of my friends was Marcus pulling Ethan away by the scruff of his shirt—as Clare pulled me away by mine.

"We have to punch through—"

"We have to run!" she yelled, above the noise and the heat and the smoke. "Or we'll die trapped!"

She was right. Reaching Atlantis was coming down to the wire, and the Renegades had to be stopped, no matter the cost, or the danger. Marcus and the others had made their decision to come here. They would live or die by that.

"Okay."

Cut off from the others, Clare ran point, and I covered her. We managed to stay on course for the Degradation, but only just. The rise and fall of the battle's tide had forced us more to the west, alongside a scraggly tree line alight with purple flames.

As we ran, I tried to keep track of the battle between the Knights and the Renegades behind me. We were on the outskirts of the conflict now, jumping over the dead and the dying. One of them reached out and grasped the cuff of my trousers, pulling me to the ground.

"Help… me…"

He was a Knight, moaning and clutching at the bloody stump where his foot used to be attached. I shook him off, stood up, and helped him up onto his good leg. "What happened here?"

The man was missing an eye. "About a thousand nightmares poured out of the Degradation, and the Renegades turned on us. I… I…" He focused on me. "Aren't you Dec—?"

A luminescent arrow pierced his neck from behind and a spray of arterial blood splashed across my face. I let him drop, and Clare pulled me away.

"Up there!" she said, pointing at the ridge about half a mile away. The very edge of the Degradation sliced the raised terrain in half, but the flag of the Dragon Throne—

the King's flag—was planted firmly against its edge. "If Faraday's there, Morpheus Renegade won't be far away."

We stayed low, argent shields spinning ever faster around us as our combined Will deflected all it could. "Do you think they're still friendly? This is a whole new game, Clare. The Tome Wars renewed!"

Clare and I ran across a small tree line, keeping to the dusky shadows as much as possible and avoiding all but the minor skirmishes of the battle.

"I don't think—" Clare stumbled, and I caught her. "Thanks. I don't think they *care*, Declan. This is about Atlantis, remember. They're both trying to breach your Degradation. I don't think they care about all these soldiers tearing themselves apart! A renewed war won't mean a damn thing if one of them takes the Lost City without the other."

"Good point."

Marcus and Sophie could look after themselves, but I was worried about Ethan and Aaron. Aaron didn't command the talent, and Ethan was only good for party tricks. With any luck, Marcus had cleared them off the field, although from my vantage point, the entire lowland seemed engulfed.

Under a hazy smoke cloud, the main fighting spread across the Plains of Perdition for a good two miles. Thick columns of smoke obscured the eastern grasslands and rose up along the edge of the Degradation. The cloud cast the dome in a purple, almost turquoise, light. Anything could be emerging unseen from the depths of the shield.

Worse than a scream is a scream cut short…

Clare and I ran towards the ridge, well clear of the main battle and a quarter mile from the rim of the Degradation. We encountered very little resistance from the scattering of soldiers below the hill. Most of them were focused on the battle.

We reached the base of the ridge below the Degradation. Moss-covered and weatherworn tombstones protruded from the earth like the teeth of an ancient and terrible beast. The cemetery was old and rose up the hillside. Some of the graves looked fresh, and were marked with the sigils of the Knights and Renegades alike.

These men and women had died here in the five years since my shield around Atlantis came into being, since I'd crippled the Story Thread. They had died because of me, to destroy the creatures seeping out of the Degradation.

"Hale!"

Breathing hard, I snapped out of my thoughts. King Renegade stood above us on the crest of the lower graveyard, alone and arrogant. He held a familiar looking dagger, stained red, in his hand. A key to Atlantis, torn from my side.

"Come on down, Morpheus!" I called. "Let's put an end to this."

Renegade snarled and slapped his free hand against his leg. Cords of fetid yellow light flew from his fingers and flowed into the ground. I cursed and shot a bolt of silver light at the mad king, but the ground shook and knocked me aside. Clare caught me, and I kept to my feet.

The grass began to *ripple* and bulge in warped, undulating waves.

"Oh dear…" I knew what Renegade had done. *Bastard.*

A third army entered the fray.

They came from below, from the shallow graves that littered the vast ridge. Rotting skeletal arms burst through the dirt and clawed for the surface.

The earth spat up a dread legion of the undead.

CHAPTER TWENTY-ONE

Fury

Fucking necromancy.

Summoning zombies, the soulless, walkers, politicians, the undead—call them what you will—was a desecration against everything I knew to be true and right. To be *just*. A primal rage, as red-hot as burning coals, descended over my vision.

Such anger, once upon a time, had scorched a city in blind arrogance. My rage that could annihilate and kill and disrupt the flow of time, a rage as raw as sin, was only intensified by the cries of Clare Valentine trying desperately to pull her leg clear of the rotting-fleshed hand rising from beneath her feet.

"What move to make next, Declan?" Renegade was laughing, still miles clear of sanity and heading straight to the heart of crazy town juggling TNT. *"Atlantis is mine!"*

His voice shuddered through my mind, and I realized a moment too late that he'd caught me in a web of compulsion, a thick, persuasive binding of Will—like the kind I'd used to send Jeff Brade spinning across the Void during the attack at my shop. Morpheus turned and fled up the hillside, leaving me pinned to the ground and unable to move.

I fought it. I hurled my Will back against his touch and gnawed at the strands of biting steel that bound me. The hold he'd placed on me, as brutal as any physical beating but somehow so much worse, like jagged hooks digging deep furrows across my brain, shook and spun.

My Will wasn't strong enough. The shambling creatures risen from below the earth surrounded me. Even if I did get free in time, I was trapped—

Firm hands, like sledgehammers, pushed me in the back and I was thrown across the tombstone-ridden dell, through the clawing arms of the undead. I slammed into the base of the ridge. The wind was knocked from my lungs, but I was clear of the disgusting creatures.

Clare had hit me with a pound of raw Will.

She saved my life and freed me from Renegade's compulsion.

Gasping for breath, I stumbled to one knee in time to see Clare's arms alight with purple fire. She swung lances of sharp energy at the onslaught... but it wasn't going to be enough. One of the creatures sank its teeth into her neck from behind, biting into the ropy scar tissue that crossed her throat.

"NO!"

I stumbled forward, firing shots of wild Will into the fray. A recently deceased Knight, stinking of death and decay, latched onto my arm in a surprisingly strong grip and pulled me round in a vicious circle.

A burst of heat energy exploded out of my palm and into the zombie's neck, severing its head. The distraction cost me. Clare had vanished from my sight, beneath a horde of the bloodthirsty creatures. I could hear her screaming.

Suddenly, I was channeling more Will than I had in five years. I was back in the wars, in truth and in heart. Twin jets of dark green fire flared from my palms, wreathing my arms in deadly flame. My skin, the only flesh immune to my power, tingled beneath the ferocity.

I danced among the dead, cutting a path toward Clare. My strength to sustain the flame waned, and I stumbled, breathing hard, spit running down my chin. I'd cleared great swaths of the creatures, but I'd not done enough. I could barely breathe, let alone reach Clare in time to save—

A voice roared behind me. "*Let her go!*"

Aaron, alone and unarmed, hurled himself, all one hundred and thirty kilograms of hefty fat, into the shambling creatures and began to tear them apart *with his bare hands*. He fought as if possessed. Something swaddled in a cloth bundle was strapped to his back.

I watched, stunned, as one of the zombies latched its teeth into his meaty bicep. With a bellow, Aaron drove his fingers into its hollow eye sockets and wrenched its rotten head from its neck.

Seeing that jarred me into action.

I leapt back into the fight, shooting short bursts of explosive light—all I could manage—into the creatures, and gave Aaron room to work. He knelt down where I'd last seen Clare and, with a wail, lifted her up into his arms and turned to run as I covered him.

Most of the damn things had been destroyed. I cleaned up the survivors stumbling in Aaron's wake as he crossed the desecrated earth, bleeding and panting. He fell to his knees against a rise in the ridge populated with swaying daffodils and carefully lowered Clare to the ground.

"Declan! Declan, you heal her!"

I took out the last shambling corpse and turned away sickened. Clare's wild screams had simmered down to something shallow and desperate, to something final. I spat out a mouthful of blood and ran to Aaron. My legs failed me when I saw Clare, writhing on the hillside.

She was unrecognizable, save for a single perfect eye that fluttered from blue, to red, to gold. My palms were lit with healing light, but I was too late. Her blood oozed from dozens of deep bites. The grass beneath her was stained a shocking shade of purple. I put a hand on the back of her neck and gently lifted her head onto my lap.

She bucked in my arms, and I whispered sweet nothings, holding her tight.

Aaron burst into tears, his massive chest heaving up and down. He seemed indifferent to his own wounds.

"Take…" Clare groaned. "Take… cake, Dec…"

"You too, sweet thing," I whispered.

Then she was gone.

Clare died in my arms under the glare of the Degradation, under the very last of my good intentions.

After a time, perhaps a minute, though it seemed stretched into an awfully long year, Aaron and I abandoned her at the base of the ridge and set off after Renegade. Our fight was no longer for Atlantis.

A king dies today, I thought. Warm tears coursed a narrow track through the blood on my face. My earlier rage became something else… something *cold*.

Shadowless.

CHAPTER TWENTY-TWO

Ruthless

"Where are the others?" I asked quietly, walking up the hill to the Degradation's edge with my fists clenched.

Aaron sniffed and wiped his eyes on a sleeve slick with blood. We were beaten and ruined before the true battle had even begun. Our efforts were madness but the kind of madness I'd been good at, back in the day. *Shoulda, woulda, coulda come alone...*

"Marcus... he fled, Declan. He tried to bring me with him, but he cannot control my Will—I have none. He took Sophie and Ethan and faded back along the Void. Back to my villa, if I properly understand your diving."

Trust Marcus...

I nodded. "Good, I suppose. He saved their lives." Sophie would be furious with him, but it was done. "I think he caused this, Aaron."

"Marcus? This battle?"

...until he gives you a reason not to.

"I think he told Renegade, or Faraday, that we were coming. When I sent him to get *Tales of Atlantis*. I think he wanted me stopped."

"But why?"

I shrugged. "He wasn't my friend, these last five years of exile. No, I think he was sent to watch me. To make sure I didn't make a move on Atlantis, and if I did... to stop me. He told Morpheus Renegade, I'm sure of it, and Renegade turned his army here against Faraday to make it that much more difficult for us to reach the Degradation."

"So... he has betrayed you."

"In a way, I suppose. But it kept Ethan and Sophie alive." Marcus had been at my side during Nightmare's Reach, and before. We had been Knights of the highest order—trained to kill and worse. "No matter. He's doing what he thinks is right."

We reached the top of the ridge at long last and found the flag of the Dragon Throne alight with orange flame. A wide-open space, grassed and covered in supplies and military vehicles from Ascension City, lay in ruin before the Degradation. The rippling indigo shield stood less than twenty meters away. From this distance, I could smell the hot and heavy stink of it, like burning plastic.

The encampment was devastated.

Jon Faraday and a cadre of Knights stood in the center of the grassy area, surrounded by dead Knights and masked Renegade soldiers. Their supplies and support vehicles had been destroyed. Of King Renegade there was no sign, but he had to have come this way, the only path to Atlantis.

"Faraday!" I called across the clearing, my voice harsh and unyielding. "Where is he?"

Faraday glanced over his shoulder. Beneath his crown, a momentary flicker of dismay at my presence crossed his features. One of his Knights bellowed something, and he turned back toward the Degradation.

A shadowy creature of torn leather skin emerged from the shimmering shield. It was a cousin of the demons that

151

attacked me in the Fae Palace. As one, the Knights still standing raised their glowing blades and cast bolts of heat and energy into the monstrosity. It went down wailing.

I jogged across the smoking earth, and as I drew closer I knew for certain where Renegade had gone.

"You should have stopped him," I whispered, staring not at Faraday but over his shoulder, at an imperfection in the mighty shield just an arm's length away.

"We were overrun here, Hale," Faraday said. He shifted his chest armor and followed my gaze. "This is your doing. You forced peace from war and now force war from peace."

A vortex in the Degradation warped the mighty shield and sucked in the construct like a drain sucking down water. The ethereal whirlpool was quiet save for clashes of bruised purple lightning and the gnashing of invisible bones.

"He went through there, didn't he?" I asked.

Faraday nodded. "He had a knife, coated in blood. Just a small dagger, really. He cut that hole and stepped in."

"There's a good chance the vortex killed him," I said aloud, mostly to myself.

"And there's a chance it didn't."

I gazed at the King of the Knights Infernal as if seeing him for the first time. "Are you asking for my help now, Jon?"

"This is your mess. We are here because of you."

I had to laugh. Even here, beneath the glare of the Degradation, old habits died hard. "So you want me to step through?" My blood had opened the way once before. I had walked *out* of this terrible shield on the night it was created. I could walk back in. It was tied to me, to my shadow lost in the Void.

"You did this. You fix it. Morpheus Renegade cannot be allowed to seize the treasures of Atlantis. The Infernal Clock... Broken quill, the Roseblade, Declan!"

Aaron shifted uncomfortably. "For Clare. Do this for Clare."

A thought came to me then—a terrifying, awesome thought. The Infernal Clock could grant life. Eternal life, if the stories were to be believed. It could bring Clare back. I had to reach it before Renegade. There was only one course of action left to me. I'd been too late to stop the mad king, but I was going back to Atlantis anyway.

To save the world?

No.

To save the girl.

"Are you coming?" I asked. Faraday shook his head. "And you think you deserve that crown?" I spat on the ground at his feet and stepped toward the wailing vortex. Before I could touch it, Aaron grasped my shoulder and pressed a wrapped bundle into my arms. I frowned in confusion and—

"It's what you asked me to hide in my basement, you fool."

My hands shook and I almost dropped the package. "I... no."

"Yes."

"But..."

Aaron sniffed. His hands were stained with Clare's blood. "Kill that monster, Declan. Be—"

"Ruthless?"

"—who you are."

Well, okay.

Steeling my resolve, I followed Morpheus Renegade into chaos unbound. The Degradation consumed me whole, and I was thrown across realities once more.

CHAPTER TWENTY-THREE

The Lost City

Stepping into the Degradation was like walking into a furnace of cool energy. A spring of spinning and flowing ice pressed in on me from all sides. The effect was startling, fresh, and altogether unnatural.

Then it began to hurt, of course.

Nothing this important could be gained easily or be won without spilling enough blood to sink the Titanic twice over.

A thousand knives of red-hot iron pierced my skin. My eyes rolled and boiled in their sockets, and a shower of molten, hissing steel drowned all thought and sense, save for the maddening, endless pain. The Degradation was on overdrive, kicked into third gear already doing a hundred miles an hour.

Yeehaw!

I rode that wave of pain across the space between worlds, rode that *motherfucker* down through the moments between seconds, and over the impossible gap in forever. It was always, *always* one helluva ride.

The world disappeared, and in its place was a *between* enchantment and a pathway of forgotten light. The road to Atlantis, the speckled road to power was suspended on a wing and a prayer. I spotted a tiny figure in the distance, hunched against the maelstrom.

Morpheus Renegade was already half a mile away. Time was different on this side. His few seconds of advantage through the gap in the Degradation had become minutes on the other side.

I set off after him, my palms ablaze with blue flame. But there were memories on that road. Scarred memories of the past and all the many wonderful mistakes I'd made were set to waylay and distract me.

"What do you think the kids will remember of the war, Tal?" I held my head in my hands, fighting a headache—a migraine of epic proportions.

"Grim-faced Knights patrolling the streets of Ascension City? The threat of attack, the sense that something's wrong with the world..." A pause. "And they'll remember you, of course, they'll remember Declan Hale. The Arbiter—the light against the dark. You'll be legend, Declan."

"No, they'll not remember it that way," Clare said, drawing deep on a warm, comforting cigar which looked out of place in her tiny, bloodstained hands. "They'll remember the sweet shops in Farvale going out of business... they'll remember school being cancelled." She shrugged. "Aye, but I suppose they'll remember you, Declan. You're the hero."

"Perhaps that's the best way to remember it," Tal said. "Better than the mass graves, the killing fields, the cost to the Knights..."

Something was rising from the pain, out of the sparkling darkness, something I'd fought so hard to see, to set the world ablaze for... what was that old line? About hopelessness, regret, and bitter angst at my existence? Oh yeah...

The odds are long. Life's unfair, and death's no better.

But you know what? Fuck the odds.

There was a great roar and an unexpected *thump* into the ground.

The sky filled with diamonds and became an ocean of twinkling stars scattered across an inferno of soft purple menace. I felt uneasy. I felt out of sorts. Death warmed up.

"I'm here." But I wasn't there. I was still floating on memory, in the worlds of the better-left-forgotten…

"Everything I do, I do it for you."

Tal glared. "Don't you dare throw Bryan Adams at me, Declan. You're better than that."

I pulled myself from the memories, from the furnaces of distant stars, and forced the searing pain back where it belonged—in the nothingness between this world and the last. The task wasn't an easy one but it was a task in which I was well versed.

I don't know how much time had slipped by, but I sat up and surveyed the old world around me. Renegade, if he had fared better through the Degradation than me, had a good head start, but *I* knew where I was going.

The ground was soft and spongy like moss. I sat halfway up a steep rise that stretched into the sky for what must have been miles. From my vantage point, I held a commanding view of the most awe-inspiring range of mountains ever conceived. The twisted peaks were covered in electric-blue snow and light cast from the spectacle far below, yet the range extended for miles and miles up toward the heavens. The peaks brushed the sky, and I wouldn't have been surprised if they pierced the upper reaches of the atmosphere.

Great crags of rock and cliff faces a dozen miles high played tricks with the eye and created a numbing sense of size that was hard to visually comprehend. Those rocks and cliffs were just the boundaries of this world inside the Degradation.

Down and away to the right, just past Atlantis itself, miles upon miles of black rock and twisted thrusts of reef, marred with burnt coral, brushed up against the Lost City. The ruined landscape was the coastline with the ocean just beyond, but those waters had long since dried up, leaving behind a terrifying, lifeless wasteland. The sight of it made me feel sick.

I turned away to behold the main event.

The Lost City of Atlantis sat far below, surrounded by natural barriers of impenetrable rock. A haze of indigo light merged with neon-blue over the outlandish architecture.

"Oh my," Tal whispered. "It looks so small, and yet..."

"It's huge," I assured her, and despite my bruised and bleeding condition, I managed a wink. "We're just far away... five miles at least."

And we had been, back then. Despite the uninterrupted view into the valley below, the commanding sight of Atlantis aglow in the evening, I was still miles up *above* the city. Halfway up a mountain that touched the stars. Far below, in warmer climes, towers that rivaled the highest skyscrapers back home, and towers that eclipsed such modern heights, looked like pinpricks scattered across an impossible terrain.

"What do you feel right now?" I asked Tal, and then laughed. "We've just escaped all true worlds, and now... behold another! What do you feel?"

"Afraid," she said, and that was enough. Fear—of a world where there could be no world. Neither Earth nor Forget nor Void.

Below lay the unknown, the *better-left-forgotten*, and we had been so small against the backdrop of this impossible place. But there wasn't just fear. No, not at all. There was *wonder*, astonishment, and all manner of conflicting emotions as the goal of not just one lifetime but more than I could fathom came into sight...

The Great Quest, done at last.

Yet above all there was pain. The pain of remembrance—*oh goddamn it*—and the pain of existence outside existence.

"Keep moving, Declan." I rubbed my legs to get them working. The piercing ride across realities, through the Degradation, had left me numb. Aaron's bundle lay on the ground a few feet away. The object within had half-fallen out of the cloth, and the pommel of a sheathed sword was revealed. With a heavy sigh, I unwrapped his terrible prize and strapped the cursed thing to my belt.

Only as a last resort, I thought, stroking the hilt of the weapon.

I headed toward the city using an old path, cobbled with broken stone and overgrown with mossy weeds. Dozens of gnarled and twisted cherry blossom trees, in full bloom, lined the path. Those trees were new. Last time I'd been here, with Tal, nothing had been living.

There was no sign of Renegade, but I kept my wits about me as I made quick time down the mountainside on the old road. He could be laying in ambush—I would be—or he could have made a run straight to the city. I didn't know which worried me more. I kept a pool of Will cupped in my palm, ready to kill.

Atlantis drew ever closer, and the city began to seem that much more real. The alien architecture and ancient design came into relief against the backdrop of the darkening sky. It looked beyond its time, for damn sure, yet most of it was in utter ruin.

The lights were on, though, so someone was home...

Towers scraped the sky, connected by clear walkways and bridges that stretched from the peak of one building to the next in the air over the city. Neon-blue lighting ran up and down the streets and throughout hundreds of the buildings. Legend held that Atlantis was fuelled by the same near-eternal source of energy that kept Ascension City aglow, powering the streets and keeping the abandoned metropolis running even after its defeat.

The legend came close.

Atlantis was powered by the Infernal Clock.

Clare's second chance. A shot at redemption for those of us who deserved no such thing.

One tower rose above all others in the heart of the city and shone like a beacon in the broken light. The dark spire was cut from the same obsidian stone as the Fae Palace and was huge, an unbroken citadel eclipsing all other structures in the dead city. Blue lights ran up the tower in a spiral—again, just like the Fae Palace—and at the very top, still far below me, a single sphere of white fire hovered above a flat plateau.

A few miles and an hour later I entered the city proper and beheld the splendor of a lost world.

The main promenade into Atlantis was a thin, narrow canyon lined with statues a hundred feet high on either side. Men, old lords and kings, glared down at me in silent judgment—the distant ire of the long dead.

From where I'd entered this realm, high up above on the mountainside, the city had looked mostly whole save for a few patches of ruin and rubble. However, as I walked the streets of Atlantis itself, the calamity and chaos that had claimed this fabled utopia became all too clear. The city was a husk, beyond all recovery.

A lot like your good self, tittered the voice in the back of my mind.

Not a building was left that wasn't marked, burnt or gouged by impossible powers lost so long ago. Dust lay inches thick along the roads and walkways. Wreckage and chunks of weatherworn stone lay within the dust, silent and accusing, covered in a thin layer of struggling, brown moss. Decaying husks of various metallic machines lay rusting where they had fallen. Shells of what could've been something akin to cars littered the roads.

I saw no bones.

The bones were the dust I waded through. The lost lives of *millions* in one, terrible night.

Yet the lights still worked, for the most part, and even in ruin the city was a wonder. A silent, mournful wonder.

"Save for the trees…"

More cherry blossoms had grown here, as well, up through the cracks in the sidewalks and twisting around streetlamps. The carpet of dust was peppered with soft petal-

159

falls, like drops of rain against a sandy beach. Hundreds of the pink blossoms lined the streets. The trees did not grow thickly enough to be called a forest but could claim such a title eventually, if given enough time.

I was weary from the walk down the mountain. The only sign of Morpheus Renegade was the fresh path through the dust ahead of me. The city was massive but silent. I should have been able to hear his boots clapping against the stone from a mile away. But no, *nada*.

Still, I could feel eyes on the back of my neck, almost as if I was walking in the Void. Eyes unseen and unfound. Was I being followed? Impossible, unless Renegade had moved behind me, and if so, who—or what—was I following through the dust trail?

"Hello?"

Someone laughed. A woman.

The sound hit me like a punch to the gut. I knew that laugh.

"Oh dear," I said, and sat down on a stone bench in an inch of ancient dust. The bench belonged to what could have been an old Atlantean pub. Even ten thousand years old, I knew a drinking house when I saw one. "Oh dear, oh dear…"

A whirlwind of vicious light dug furrows in the ground. A barrage of tiny yet fierce lightning strikes scorched the stone. Flames ran through the dust, quickly exhausting their fuel. Within that column of spiraling and wild light a shadowed and terrible form took shape. A woman emerged from the vortex and stepped lightly across the space between us on delicate bare feet.

Tal Levy took my hand and brought it up to her lips, planting a soft kiss on my palm.

She stared at me with eyes the color of blood.

"Hey there, songbird," I said. "Of all the bars in all the world…"

CHAPTER TWENTY-FOUR

...*Is New Again*

Apart from those blood-red eyes, twin orbs of crimson enchantment, Tal was as beautiful as I remembered. More so, due to the length and breadth of time that had passed since I'd watched her die. Her olive skin, her dark hair, her gentle smile upon a face of soft angles... God, I had *missed* this girl.

"Come close." She leaned in her head as she touched my forearm with both her hands. Her touch was insubstantial, frail and weak, as if she was doing all she could to hold herself together and tethered to reality. Her touch was almost too much.

I felt her breath, warm and fresh on my face. The lilt of her voice, the yielding accent of her Israeli birthplace, was so familiar, but her scent was what made her presence real. A mix of citrus and primrose. The smell of winter becoming spring.

"I'm sorry," I said. "I am truly sorry."

"Oh, don't you apologize, Declan Hale. It makes me think you've done something wrong."

"If I could rewrite it. Go back and change..." A small smile touched my lips. "Well, coulda, woulda, shoulda, songbird. Our first time would never have been to a Dire Straits song, I'll tell you that much."

"You can't, and you wouldn't. We both know that. I made my choices here, and so did you."

"It was supposed to be... That fucking god *tricked* me." Tears half a decade old blurred my vision. I blinked them away. "Tal, you still exist. You're here. I can find a way to bring you back. The Infernal Clock can grant eternal life."

Tal smiled. "Only if there's a body, and you're kneeling in what's left of mine."

"No, I don't accept that. I *refuse* that."

"Would you bargain again with Lord Oblivion?" Tal's smile turned forlorn. "Declan, would you dare? After the last time? But what have you left to trade, hmm? Certainly not your shadow. Your soul, perhaps? Damn yourself to grant me something I gladly gave up."

"I need you with me."

"You *need* nothing and, to be honest, deserve even less."

I knew the truth when I heard it. Tal never lied, not ever, which was what made her so wonderful. Her words mirrored my thoughts. She knew me so well. I let her frail hand fall and clenched my fists. "I have a request."

"That's why you are still alive and the armies of Ascension City are not. You never push, do you, Declan? You move so carefully, with such faux confidence, such dangerous charm. You request when you could so easily demand."

"Tal, our choices five years ago are killing Forget. The Story Thread is unraveling, and travesties from the Void and beyond are seeping into all worlds. It's my fault, and I will not endure another bloodbath. Can you do anything to stop the Degradation?"

"I am the Degradation." Tal's form shimmered and moved around me like a blizzard of living sparks. "My life force feeds the shield around the Lost City. You would unmake all that I am?"

"I would. Time's up, honey. Better a renewed war between the Knights and the Renegades, don't you think, than the end of so many worlds?"

Tal snarled and her crimson eyes flared. She drew a small dagger from her belt and slashed it across my face. I snapped my head back a moment too late, and the blade cut across my cheek and along the bridge of my nose. The pain was real enough. Blood ran in rivulets into my mouth.

"I exist outside of this world—of all worlds. Your request is denied, Knight. In the words of one far greater than you: *You shall not pass*." Her voice deepened at the last of her words, becoming something far older and crueler. Perhaps my Tal was here, but she wasn't alone. Those red eyes…

Oblivion was *watching*, the Voidling had said back in Perth. Another piece of the puzzle fell into place.

Tal took a deep breath and calmed herself. She sheathed her tiny, vicious dagger and cupped my bloody cheek. "There, there now. I'm sorry." She ran her fingers along the deep cut, and I felt the skin tingle and stretch. "That's better."

The bleeding had stopped. I pushed her hand aside and felt the skin for myself. The cut was a week old at least, and was healing. My mind flashed back to my death… I'd had a scar just like this—recent, raw, but mending.

"How did you do that?" I asked.

She licked my blood from her fingers. "Time is… Well, time can be persuaded here. Atlantis exists in a crux, powered and held by the Infernal Clock, and hidden ten thousand years in the past."

"This is the past?"

"One of many, and only a small shard of the whole."

"Oh, Tal." I'd always thought she was special. "You're not my Tal anymore. I'm sorry. So, so sorry… last time counts for all. I give my love to whatever is left of you behind those eyes."

She giggled. "Depart this place or perish, Shadowless—"

I drew the sword at my waist, and it flared to life with ethereal brilliance—the silver light from my Will. The single, flawless diamond in its hilt shone against the purple sky and sparkled with radiance found. Tal leapt back but not quickly enough. With a whimper, I drove my sword into the glimmering ghost and scattered all that she was, and the eyes of a god, into the ether.

The Roseblade *sang*.

She, whoever she was, would be back, given the delight I saw in those heart's-blood orbs.

I didn't have much time, even in this land that time forgot.

CHAPTER TWENTY-FIVE

The Infernal Clock

Five years ago, on the eve of the Degradation, Tal and I had run these ruined streets together, ahead of the Knights and the Renegades. We had run hard and fast, desperate to seal away the chaos we'd found and unleashed.

The Infernal Clock and the promise of immortality.

The Roseblade that had destroyed Reach City.

Well, no, that didn't own the madness—not even close. I'd destroyed the city by using the Roseblade, which was a tool of intent, after all. My doing. Eight million dead and a corner of Forget turned into a horrendous monument to the power found in the Lost City—all my doing.

The race had been on that night. Everyone thought I'd left the Roseblade sealed away inside the Degradation alongside the Infernal Clock. I'd sealed it away all right, inside a simple chest and given it to Aaron. Half the reason I'd grudgingly accepted my exile was because the temptation to use the sword again would have been too strong.

I would have cut a vicious, bloody path through Ascension City and seized the Dragon Throne. As you do when you're young, I guess.

As much as I detested Faraday's kingship and his laws barring me from Forget, after Nightmare's Reach I'd been shaken enough to see that gaining the throne with the Roseblade was insane. I'd thought Clare was dead, and I'd *known* Tal was dead… no one could have stopped me.

Except myself.

At least I'd forced an end to the Tome Wars.

I'd buried the damned sword and accepted Faraday's exile. Better a defeated fool than a victorious monster.

I couldn't make up for what I'd done and the lives I'd destroyed. The Degradation was a mistake, but at the time, necessary, and here we all were, Knights, Renegades, and my merry band, fighting over this husk of a city once more.

My face hurt where Tal had cut me.

Sweet like cinnamon, that one, I thought as I ran through the streets paved with dust and strewn with cherry blossom petals.

Tal's favorite flower.

Of Morpheus Renegade I had lost all sign. His footsteps, if indeed they had been his, had petered out. I gazed up at the mile-high skyscraper, a spire of obsidian rock smoothed and shining under the twilit sky. *Are you up there, you bastard?* He would die for what he'd done to Clare, even if I brought her back with the Clock. He would die for so much more, as well. Some men just needed killing, and Renegade was long overdue on his butcher's bill. The weapon of mass destruction strapped to my waist would see to it, if nothing else. I patted the Roseblade and headed into the dark, all-consuming tower. *God, I hope it didn't come to that…*

Inside was a large open space of sharp shadows and little else, at the heart of which rose an impressive set of steps, spiraling up in loops through the ceiling and into the tower beyond. I made for that staircase, panting and dreading the climb to come. I would've traded the Roseblade for a sip of liquid courage.

"Last piece of the puzzle," I muttered, climbing the mighty spiral staircase. Torches of blue light, centuries old but inscribed with runes of power, spluttered and died on the walls as I passed.

My death was falling into place. I wore the right clothes and bore the correct scarring across my face from Tal's handiwork. All I was missing was the gaping wound in my stomach.

A wiser man would've been running in the other direction. But I'd never been mistaken for wise, and what was it the Historian had said? *You have to be brave.*

Well, so be it. Although there was nothing brave about what I had planned for Renegade, when we caught up.

I don't know how long I climbed in the dark, but eventually the spiral staircase ended in a wide and gloomy space, lit only by Atlantis's terrible sky, the inner curve of the Degradation, through long-shattered windows. In the center of the room was a high-backed stone seat, carved from the same rock as the tower. Another throne from another time.

Now that I was here again, I was sure of it. Ascension City had been founded on some faint, lost memory of Atlantis. The blueprints were nearly identical.

Beyond the throne was a final set of stairs rising up behind a pair of dilapidated and cracked golden gates. Tal and I had forced our way through those gates once upon a time. At the top of that staircase we'd found the Roseblade, seen the Infernal Clock, and bartered with a creature of such power that it could rightly be called a god.

Nothing for it, Dec. Keep moving. Time to put an end to all the warring and power plays before anybody else died for the ambition of selfish men.

I moved past the throne and through the old gates. Last time I'd been here, I'd lost so much and gained so little. A moment's hesitation was all I could afford. Weary and hurting, I climbed the last hurdle and reached the top of the staircase, the end of the road.

Wind whistling through my hair, I looked out at the Lost City and the miles of dead ocean, surrounded by those impossibly tall mountains. The wall of the Degradation sizzled above it all.

I stood atop a wide and broken plateau, gazing up at that sky strewn with heavy violet clouds that sped across the atmosphere as fast as Willed fire. A storm of cherry blossom petals had been swept up into the heavens. They fell like snow and choked the world.

A fetid stink of sulphur clung to the air. The ground beneath my feet was cracked and *breathing*. Arcs of red light, like magma, burned within the stone. The roots of the Infernal Clock splintered out from the center of the plateau. The Clock grew on a dais that overlooked the abyss of Atlantis.

A curious place to find a crystal rose.

"But then a rose is a rose is a Rose," I whispered and stepped forward toward that beautiful chasm, the end of the road, the white flower of moment—the Infernal Clock.

All that I had done or ever did, was to gain this moment under the burnt sky, amidst the dust and the fire and the dew-speckled petals of Time.

To save the Story Thread.

To reignite the Infernal Works.

Above all, and most recent, to bring Clare back to life.

Memories came to me of Tal and the last time I was here. Always the understanding, the knowledge, the know-how of the universe, was thrust through my mind.

Years ago, the Everlasting Lord Oblivion had barred our path to the rose. I was alone this time. The gods outside of creation did not seem to care that I'd made it this far again. Perhaps that should have worried me, but my desire to see Clare remade washed all worry away.

I could feel the Clock ticking inside my head like a song—a terrible song of Forget, which sounded a lot like Springsteen circa 1975. *Broken heroes just born to run*. Or something. It ticked away, second between second, and I understood what it was saying, singing, *screaming*.

"I hear ya…"

I touched the Infernal Clock—perhaps the first to do so in the history of this and *any* universe—and was dashed to pieces on a landscape of such immense size that it dwarfed distant stars and the black space between distant stars. The truth of reality *wasn't* distance, but size. In a shade of a moment I was pulled and wrenched in both inner and outer space, across galaxies of fire and within atoms of ice. I saw worlds end and begin in rage. I saw how little humanity understood existence. We were children. Ants. Playing with the ascending oils of creation crashing on the shores of an endless beach.

And I was not even a grain of sand on that beach. I was not even the smallest fraction of a grain of sand on that beach.

I wept. My irrelevance was infinite.

CHAPTER TWENTY-SIX

The Infinite Sadness

Tal wrapped her arms around my chest as I sagged to my knees. She was a ghost of a memory and couldn't hold my weight. She slumped down with me and rested her head on my back. All things being even, she had reassembled herself in record time, but then was that so surprising, really, after everything else?

"I tried to warn you, Declan. You were never meant to listen, though."

"There's so much… *nothing*. We're dancing on a sheet of thin ice over a precipice of… of chaos and nightmare. Always. All the time. Even the Void is just a stretched canvas… Tal, I…"

I was wracked with harsh sobs. If Tal hadn't been less than smoke, my heaving chest would have shaken her loose.

"Hush now." She giggled and the sound was not even *close* to human anymore, more like nails on a chalkboard.

"I don't want to know. It's too much. *Take it back!*" I spat at the Rose, the Infernal Clock, and it glittered with indifference. Tal's laughter was infectious. I laughed too, though the sound was indistinguishable from garbled cries.

Time trickled on, as it does—even in the heart of Atlantis—and I slowly came back to some semblance of sanity. I shook away the vestiges of what the Clock had shown me. Eternity, or something like it. A glimpse of the infinite sadness made real. A glimpse of chaos unbound. The knowledge had almost driven me over the edge, screaming into the blissful nothing. But no—not yet.

Work still to be done, boss.

I may have been less than an insignificant speck on the face of an immense and cold universe, but I still found meaning, hidden in lost shadows and pieces of cake. I mattered to me. Tal mattered to me, what was left of her. Sweet Clare. There were people I cared for, people who had purpose. Sophie, Ethan, and Aaron, just to name a few. Emily Grace, back on True Earth, to name one more.

There may have been no meaning in the very large—existence was mindless chaos—but the Clock could not erase meaning from the very small.

I leveled the Roseblade against the golden-green stem of the Infernal Clock. The thud of rushed, clapping footsteps sounded behind me. A long, harrowing cry for mercy echoed throughout my skull. I heeded it not.

"*No!*" Morpheus Renegade screamed across the vast plateau.

I severed the spine of all that ever was, and all that ever could be—born within those blasted, those awful, those dum-de-de-dum-dum… distant stars.

The Clock screamed as I cut it in half.

But then the Clock would, being the complainin' fateful *sumabitch* that it was. I needed the petals—to bring Clare back—and severing the Clock was the only way to unmake the Degradation.

The scream rode the edge of the wind, and, for all I knew, echoed across the vast, bountiful realms of Forget. A near-silent scream of mercy unheeded, of regretful fury. The radiance of the petals seemed to die as my sword passed through the fragile, timeless stem.

I caught the Clock before it fell to the barren rock, while Tal's terrible laughter echoed in my ears. The thorns cut my fingers and lacerated my palm. The pain stung like all hell, but considering the crime against creation I'd just committed, the pain was bearable.

The ground began to shake. Torrents of liquid flame burst forth through the dust across the harsh horizon, setting alight the blizzard of blossom petals. The sky ignited—a million *million* petals caught alight. The rose was heavier than it should have been—*worlds heavier, boss.* It shook in my grasp, in its death throes. I quickly sheathed the Roseblade to hold the Clock steady with both hands.

It was over and I had won. But the cost, as always, was a defeated victory. With Atlantis's power source severed, the Degradation would disperse, there was that, and the Story Thread would recover, given enough time.

"You… you utter fool."

I turned and stared at Morpheus Renegade. He was ashen and shaking, stumbling toward me with arms outstretched. Foamy blood and spit oozed from his mouth and ran down his chin. He was insane—I could sense it, smell it on him as if it were a disease. Perhaps I hadn't beaten him here, after all.

"You touched it, didn't you?" I asked, gesturing with the Infernal Clock. "It drove you mad."

"Do you know what you've done? *What you've unmade?*" He drew a long, thin rapier from the sheath at his belt. His once-shiny armor was splattered with gore and coated in slick dust.

I raised a glowing palm. "Stop."

His sword shimmered and thick coils of dark flame spun around the metal, narrowing to a slender point. "You think to command *me,* Hale? This is my city—that is *my* prize. *Give it to me!*"

He thrust his blade forward and a ball of crackling energy burst across the space between us. I waved my hand and deflected the bolt skywards, into the fray above. The burnt orange sky was tearing itself apart now, and glimpses of fresh blue firmament were seeping in. Atlantis was falling through time, as the Degradation died.

Renegade and I fought, moving back and forth across the plateau. In one hand, I held the Infernal Clock and in the other, a pool of luminescent smoke.

In my mind, there was only one thought, one urge: *Kill.*

Clare's dried blood on my hands and in my clothes drove that urge.

I embraced it.

Renegade moved in close, swinging his slim sword and howling for my head. He closed the gap between us, making it next to impossible to fire off a shot of Will, as all my time was used to weave between his deadly blows. A large man, but old, Renegade used his size to force me toward the edge of the plateau.

I tried to redraw the Roseblade, but was too slow.

Renegade's hand closed around my arm, and he pulled me harshly to the side as he reached for the crystal rose. I slammed my fist into his face, cracking my knuckles, and we separated. His blade cut a thin line through my shirt and across my chest. A line of blood blossomed through the fabric.

"Ha!" Renegade roared, sensing an advantage.

I ducked low as he swung in again, and I slammed the pommel of the Roseblade against his leg as I drew the crystal sword, dropping him onto one knee against the stone. He whipped his sword around, aiming for my neck, but I lunged back a step.

Our blades caught—the Roseblade cut through his weapon like a hot knife through butter.

His rapier shattered, and Renegade was left holding a hilt attached to a few inches of warped steel. He looked stunned.

I sensed *my* advantage—

Tal giggled.

—and drove the Roseblade through his chest plate and into his heart.

The enchanted sword slipped through the king with little resistance. I snarled, breathing hard, and forced the cool crystal to the hilt into his chest. Two feet of bloody blade thrust from his spine. Renegade fell back with me atop of him, driving us both down onto the plateau. The Roseblade cut through the stone and pinned him to the tower.

His arm, still clutching his ruined rapier, jerked up and pierced my belly with three inches of blunt, melted steel.

Oh.

A torrent of hot pain blossomed, like so many roses unfurling, and ran up my side.

Shit.

"That was for Clare..." I groaned, rolling off Renegade and pulling his broken rapier, embedded in my gut, with me.

I struggled a bit with the blade, but that only turned the stinging pain into something sharper, so I stopped.

I stood but immediately fell to my knees, as men pierced by swords are wont to do.

A glimmer of satisfaction seemed to shine in Morpheus Renegade's eyes, and then nothing shone there, save the reflected bursts from the reality storm bombarding the city.

Grinning like a lunatic, Renegade died first, pierced upon the Roseblade atop the highest point of the highest tower in the Lost City of Atlantis.

"Good riddance," I said and yanked his sword from my stomach with a cry that sent me reeling away across the plateau in blinding agony.

Wounded but still clutching the crystal rose, I watched Tal's ghostly form approach me. Her smile was gentle and sure. Vicious rips in the very seams of reality crackled like lightning across the sky and through the burning ash fall. I was heading full circle toward death, the puzzle all but complete.

Tal half-caught me and half-dropped me on the very edge of the Infernal Clock's ruined dais. I could see down over the edge, into the sharp vortexes—the reality storms. I was catching glimpses into the Void. Perhaps there would be nothing left, once the Degradation dispersed completely, and Atlantis was thrust back into proper time, onto the Plains of Perdition. That was a happy thought.

"Here you are at the end, Declan. Was it as good for you as it was for me?"

Her pale hands found their way to my side, attempting to stem the flow from the sword wound. My blood seeped *through* her flesh, slow but steady. I couldn't look into her crimson orbs.

"Did you want this to happen?"

Lord Oblivion smiled through Tal's eyes. "Now you're catching on."

I moaned and closed my eyes, still clutching the Clock which was supposed to grant eternal life. So why was I dying slowly with nothing but the shade of a lover and one of the Everlasting for company?

"Have I done more harm than good here today?" I asked the unseen god.

"That remains to be seen, Knight. You have forced change after ten thousand years of relentless stagnation. The barriers between Forget and True Earth should fall. Creatures not seen in the genuine universe since the Dawn of Moment are stirring." It paused. "So you may rest now. Do not fight the eternal sleep. Die well in the knowledge that, for the smallest fraction of time, you held the greatest power in all creation. The power to destroy it."

"I'd rather a glass of scotch, between you and me." I tried to laugh but coughed up a little more blood instead. "Let me speak to her."

Oblivion paused, perhaps contemplating my request. "As you wish." Some of the blood seemed to fade from her eyes.

Tal stared at me and said nothing. Could she really hear me? Or was the Everlasting just playing games? After everything, did it make any difference if it was her or not? Tal's death, my death, the battles lost and won. All things said and done, what could I possibly say that would hold even the smallest scrap of purpose or meaning? Goodbye, of course. Goodnight, sweetheart. We were just lonely rivers flowing to the sea, to the sea.

"Did you see a future for us, Tal?" I asked, but she only stared. "Did you see us waking up together? Smiling in the morning? Did you see us laughing and growing old? Did you see me loving you even more for every morning as the years flew past?" I took a deep breath and exhaled slowly. "Boy, I sure did."

A sigh that was more of a wince brought me close to tears.

"Please say something."

An arc of wicked purple lightning tore the heavens apart.

"Oh well. Songbird, I love—"

Tal pressed an ethereal finger against my lips. Her eyes, the eyes of a Knight, blurred from harsh crimson to soft, pepper brown. For a heartbeat, or the moment between, she was mine again in mind, body, and soul.

"I know," she whispered, and vanished like smoke on the wind.

All things said and done in truth.

The world didn't end, after all, but that did not seem so important under the burning cobalt sky.

~~*~*

Dying alone now, I had time to think about all that happened. What made sense and what did not.

Lord Oblivion had played a long game, it seemed, forcing me back here with a *need* to destroy the Infernal Clock. I never would have done that five years ago, not for anything. But to stop the Degradation and save the Story Thread... The Everlasting had played me like a fiddle. I'd done exactly what It wanted. And now the consequences were unknown and unfathomable.

You have forced change...

I sure had.

The pain in my side was fatally grim but bearable. I had a view away to my left of the city, of the reality storm forcing it through the ruins of the Degradation and across time to the Plains of Perdition. All my work was undone, but for the right reasons. To my right, Morpheus Renegade still grinned at me from where he was pinned to the stone by the Roseblade.

"Quit smiling, you bastard."

My vision blurred, but I caught movement from the far side of the plateau. I tried hard to focus. Someone, dressed all in white, emerged from the staircase that led down into the spire. A tall person, familiar.

She moved across the tower—purposeful, soundless footsteps—and paused when she reached Renegade. Carefully, she closed his eyes with her hand and ran her fingers along the golden hilt of the blade stuck through his heart, and then continued on to me. I thought about playing dead, but I was close enough to the real thing to make little difference.

The Immortal Queen lowered herself to her knees next to me and brushed my blood-soaked fringe out of my eyes. She sighed and removed her mask.

"Oh… you bad girl."

Beholding the face behind the porcelain, I felt all the blades—real and emotional—dig and twist just a little deeper. I was still alive enough to feel like an idiot.

"Would you like a sweet?" Emily Grace asked, offering me a bag of strawberry bonbons.

"No, thank you." I took a shallow breath and kept a hand pressed against the wound in my side. "I'm sweet enough."

"You killed my husband."

"I told all of you that I would, in Ascension City."

"Yes… but he has killed you, too."

A lot of things fell into place, through the hazy pain. "I suppose you were the one who left *Tales of Atlantis* on the beach for me to find. Was it only half a week ago I watched you dance at Paddy's? How did I not know it was you, Emily?"

The Immortal Queen shrugged as she rested one hand on the small roundness of her belly, her unborn son, if prophecy was to be believed. "You didn't want me to be anything but what I was. A friend, someone to flirt with, and the promise of something more." She *tsked*. "Declan, you don't get to have that."

"No, I suppose not." I unclenched my fist and let the Infernal Clock fall. It struck the obsidian plateau with a dull chime. "Same old mistakes, hmm. Brand new ways. Like loving a woman you can't have… hoping for a future that will never come."

"The eternal trap of desire, yes?"

The Clock petals unfurled and fell from the bud of the flower like the shards of a broken glass. "Will you… will you take one of those to Clare Valentine? Bring her back, please. She didn't deserve to die. Not like that."

Emily glanced at the crystal flower stem, hunger in her eyes, and snatched it up. She stood, gazing just beyond me at the city ablaze, a mile below. "Is that what you want, Declan? A last request?"

Her face was blank—she may as well have been wearing her mask again. "It is," I said carefully. "Please."

She glanced back at Renegade, then back at me. "Then it gives me great pleasure to see you die unsatisfied, Shadowless."

The Immortal Queen jammed her heel into my wound and, with a cry of exultant triumph, kicked me over the edge of the plateau and into the open air a mile above the burning city. Petals from the Infernal Clock scattered as I snatched at her foot and missed.

I fell.

I fell hard and fast, the wind rushing past my ears and stinging my eyes. Like a ragdoll, sodden and bloody, I fell through burning cherry blossoms riding the edge of the reality storms.

The ground rushed up to meet me in a final embrace—

A bolt of sizzling silver light, a strike from one of the tears in reality, struck me in the chest a split second before I was splattered in the dust. My entire form convulsed, and Atlantis disappeared.

The Void consumed me.

CHAPTER TWENTY-SEVEN

Bad Girls, Honey

"Declan! Declan Hale, help me out here…"

I lay on a cool wooden floor. The scent of musky vanilla, cut grass, and old leather washed over me, mingled with the harsh copper tang of blood. Here I was at the end, back at the beginning.

Dying on the floor of my shop.

"Don't keep me waiting, pretty boy."

I rolled over onto my back and groaned as I tried to piece it all together. The reality storms ravaging Atlantis, the death throes of the Infernal Clock, had spat me through the Void and *time*. Back here, to True Earth and to the start of all this madness—my death just over a week ago, as I understand events.

Declan Hale, ugly son of a bitch that he was, gazed at me from above. I was looking up at myself.

"Stop staring, sweetheart," I said, and grinned one *helluva* bloody grin.

He reached out his hand to touch me, which was just too weird.

"Don't touch me—you'll create a paradox that'll destroy the universe."

He snatched his arm back. "Really?"

"No. Not really. But you touch yourself enough as it is." I laughed. How long did it take to die? Not much longer, if memory served. "I just wanted... wanted to tell you something." I let go of my wound and motioned him in closer. His breath was warm and stank of old scotch.

"You're me?" he asked.

"And you will be me."

"How long before this happens?"

"You got just over a week. Grim forests in the dark, Dec." What could I tell him that would make a difference? The truth of what was to come? The knowledge of my death hadn't saved me. No, events had played their course.

Destiny cast no shadow.

"I can't save you from that wound. All the Will in the world couldn't... Are you wearing my favorite grey waistcoat?" he asked.

"It looks better on me," I said. "And we both know I don't deserve saving. We're dead, Dec." There was very little pain anymore. I felt almost... euphoric. At peace, after so long. Perhaps saying goodbye to Tal had done that. "Now listen. I am you. This is real. Call it time travel if it helps you sleep at night. It won't, trust me, but it'll keep you alive for... heh... for now."

"What are you—?"

"Shut up and listen." I could tell myself the important things and save as much as I knew how to save. At least the Degradation would be undone this way. Nothing was more important than that. Not my life. Not even Clare's. "Train Ethan, love Clare, hug Sophie. *Forgive* the Historian. And trust Marcus, until he gives you a reason not to. And he will, oh my yes, he will."

The rest of the track was just a sad song stuck on repeat, baby. I kept thinking of Emily, back in Atlantis. She had the

Infernal Clock and the Roseblade. It didn't matter, I suppose. This was my death, only moments away.

Younger Declan had a rough week ahead of him. He leaned down and looked as though he had something to say, so I lunged up and wrapped a hand around his neck, pressing our foreheads together to cut him off. He had a lot to understand, and there wasn't very much I could tell him, just enough to die kind of satisfied.

"Don't be such an arrogant *fuck*," I growled. "And get a haircut. This ain't no painted desert serenade." Was that everything? Things were getting dark now. *Low road, boss.* It didn't hurt so much anymore. "Something else… something… Ah, yeah. Declan, remember, Tal *always* aimed for the heart."

I had enjoyed seeing her, what had been left behind, and seeing a lot of familiar things and friends this last week. Oh well.

All the meager strength I had left fled my limbs, and I fell back. My head hit the floor with a sickening thud.

Someone turned out all the lights.

CHAPTER TWENTY-EIGHT

The Madman's Lullaby

Of dying, I remember very little.

It hurt—then it didn't.

Of waking up, I remember every second.

It hurt—and did not *stop* hurting.

I've had some hangovers in my time, seen a few empty scotch bottles scattered across the room and more than one or two half-eaten kebabs, but this was something else entirely.

I opened my eyes to a world of pain and drew in a harsh, startled breath that filled my lungs with what felt like a mix of ice water and acid.

Some part of me felt strong hands holding me down as I thrashed and moaned.

Blinding light made me blink rapidly and fight whatever was holding me back. Whoever was restraining me was just a dark silhouette against the glare.

"Be still, Hale."

The voice echoed as if from a great distance. I moaned, fighting through the pain, and did my best not to struggle. I hurt too much to move. After a time that may have been five minutes, or longer, I could make out more than a hazy shadow. A simple, plain room came into stark focus: a worn carpet, walls in need of paint, and a single hanging halogen bulb swinging in the breeze that came through an open window.

"Where?" I groaned.

"You're above the kebab shop in Riverwood Plaza, Hale. True Earth, just across from your shop. My humble abode these last few weeks."

Old Mathias, the banana cart salesman, held me down. His lip was split from where I must have hit him.

"Mathias?" I blinked, trying to work through it all. I remembered Clare, Atlantis, the Infernal Clock, Renegade, and Emily. "How? How are you here? Are we both dead?"

"Far from it, my friend," he said with a chuckle. His accent was gone and his grasp of English much improved.

I'd been tricked. "Who are you, then? Really?"

"We've met before, you and I. More than once." Mathias dabbed at his lip with a handkerchief. "Before you destroyed Reach City. I cut the throat of one of your allies to draw you out."

Clare. He was talking about sweet Clare.

My head was killing me. "Jade?" It couldn't be. He looked so old, so worn. Jade had only been in his fifties five years ago. He had been an enemy on both sides in the Tome Wars, after forsaking a position at the Infernal Academy. If I remembered correctly, his wife had been murdered, and Jade had turned cold. A homicidal maniac, a mercenary for hire to the highest bidder. "Aloysius Jade...?"

Jade inclined his head. "At your service."

"What happened to you?"

"Well, I didn't die, as you did, but I came close. Five years in Starhold can nearly kill a man."

I shook my head, disbelieving. "We were this close to one another on the street. I ate one of your damned frozen bananas, and I didn't recognize you."

"My own mother, bless her cruel heart, wouldn't recognize me now. I'm an old man, in body if not mind." He shrugged. "Aren't you curious?"

"Curious?"

"About why you're alive."

I shrugged, then sat up, holding my belly. The devastating stab wound in my stomach, from Renegade's sword, was a mess of tangled scar tissue. It looked nasty but old. I felt my face. Tal's cut was a thin, soft line running down my nose.

I was healed.

Alive and healed.

"No, I'm pretty sure I know what happened." I held my head in my hands for a long moment. Memories returned to me about being on the plateau of the Infernal Clock. As Emily, the Immortal Queen, had kicked me from the summit I'd snatched wildly at her foot... and missed. But I'd managed to clutch a single petal before I fell.

"It was the Infernal Clock that brought me back. Had to be. What I don't understand is why you're here, why you're... *caring* for me." I thought about it. "No, I'm sorry. I just don't get it."

"A petal of the Infernal Clock... Legend says such a thing can grant immortality."

"Do I look immortal?"

He snorted. "You look like death warmed up."

I pressed a hand to my forehead and sniffed. "That's funny. I think I need a drink."

Jade produced a bottle of red wine and two glasses. "From your own selection, of course. To your good health, hmm."

We drank in silence. I could only sip at the rose-red liquid.

"The petal was glowing and embedded in your palm, when I found you—your body, I mean—in what's left of the Reach." Jade paused. "I invoked a dash of Will into it, then a touch more. I used all the Will I had, and I haven't been able to so much as channel a drop since, but the petal began to *sing*. I felt… I felt very small."

"You saw me dispose of my body a week ago, didn't you?"

"I've been watching you for weeks, Hale. Renegade broke me out of Starhold and sent me to either drag you back to Forget or kill you trying, and bring back a vial of your blood." He shrugged. "I guess he got tired of waiting, and sent that kid to break your exile and force you to act. Morpheus is not the patient type."

"*Was* not the patient type. He's dead. I killed him." Jade, for the first time, looked surprised. "But you avoided my question. The night I… I died?"

"Yes, I saw you. I felt the cords of Will you used to send the body—I didn't know it was your own, at this point—across to Nightmare's Reach. Honestly? I was curious. You have racked up a more than significant death toll, Hale, so why so much trouble to hide one more? I went searching in the Reach, followed the thread of your Will through the dust to that house."

"And brought me back."

"And brought you back."

"I suppose I should thank you…"

Jade shook his head slowly. "We owe each other no thanks."

~~*~*

My shop door was unlocked and the books undisturbed. Jade had collected his meager possessions just after noon and left me to rise or fall of my own accord. His—Mathias's—old banana cart leaned forlornly and abandoned in the heart of Riverwood Plaza.

Entering my shop did not feel like coming home as returning to Ascension City had seemed. As time flew, I had died ten days ago on this shop floor and just two days ago in Atlantis. I had difficulty wrapping my head around all that had happened, but then the very idea of time travel was absurd.

If time flew as straight as an arrow, then I had been dead a little less than forty-eight hours.

I stood in the half-light which seeped through the cracks in the boarded up windows. Dust particles danced across the leather-bound tomes. I stroked the scar tissue on my palm where the petal of immortality had pierced me and brought me back to life.

"Roper? Detective? Are you here?"

Silence.

Could I go back to this? To my exile and this shop, to drink away the days writing an endless story? Did I have a say in the matter? Did Forget know I was dead? What had happened to Atlantis and my friends upon the Plains of Perdition?

Too many questions. Perhaps I should have just been thankful to be alive when so many weren't. I had failed Clare, as I had failed Tal. Marcus had been right all along, and on some level, I'd known that for the truth.

Only the guilty understand the cost of true power, Aaron had said. He'd got that right.

I headed upstairs for a shower and a change of clothes. The shirt and waistcoat I wore felt as though they belonged to a dead man. I spent a good hour under the scalding hot water, trying very hard not to beat my head against the tiled wall.

In my closet was a row of fresh shirts and trousers. I selected a black waistcoat and, given the torn and bloodied state of my grey one, bestowed the coat with the dubious honor of "favorite". I shrugged into it carefully, being careful to not pull too much at the taut, hard skin across my stomach.

Now what?

Being alive… it didn't feel real, somehow. I felt as though I was waiting for the other shoe to drop. Yawning, I sat down on the edge of my bed and thought of Clare. I remembered her, just a week ago, getting dressed here in a shaft of sunlight. She had been beautiful.

Distantly, I heard the bell above my door downstairs chime as someone let themselves in. I hadn't locked it behind me, and the wards weren't up. Was it someone come to hurt me, or just a customer?

I grabbed a copy of Figley's *Assassin,* the very same Jeffrey Brade had tried to use against me, and headed downstairs.

The shop was quiet. I couldn't see anyone.

Barefooted, I stepped lightly along the floorboards. "Who's here?" I asked, my voice a harsh whisper. "Show your—"

Sophie barreled into me at top speed when I rounded the edge of the shelves. Her tiny weight almost sent me tumbling over a stack of fiction, but I caught myself against the wall. "Well, hello there, 'Phie."

"I thought you were dead, you idiot!"

"I… was."

Sophie swatted me on the chest. "Where've you been? What happened? I'm sorry we couldn't help you—Marcus, he pulled us back across to Ascension City and then here. He burned *Tales of Atlantis,* Declan. Without it we—"

"It's okay. I know. He did what he thought was right and probably saved your lives." Selling me out to Renegade and plunging Forget back into war as well, but that was revenge for another time. "Are you okay? Is Ethan?"

"Ethan? Yes, he's fine. He's at university." Sophie looked at me. *Really* looked at me. "God, you look so unwell. Come and sit down."

I didn't argue. She led me over to my comfortable window alcove and sat me down in front of the typewriter. A half-written page hung in its teeth. Writing was the farthest thing from my mind.

"Declan, please, what happened?"

I looked into Sophie's face and shrugged. She deserved to know that I saw Tal again, if nothing else. I told her everything. She sat and listened, with her legs tucked underneath her on the leather sofa. She listened quietly, scared, and I could see a thousand questions blazing behind her eyes. I finished and reached for a bottle of scotch.

"You were dead," she said.

"Yes."

"You saw Tal."

"Oh yes."

Sophie looked down and bit her lip.

"Were you expecting something else? Something more?" I chuckled, but it hurt. "For all of us to live happily ever after?"

"Is that silly?"

"No. A touch naïve, perhaps, but in the best way." I stood, joined Sophie on the sofa, and slipped an arm around her shoulders to pull her close. "Perfect endings... they don't exist, 'Phie. Only in stories, where nothing ever really changes. Here, right now, isn't a story. There is no happy ending, because it's not the end. Do you understand?"

Sophie sniffed and placed her hand on my knee. "I miss Tal."

Me too.

~~*~*

A day later, the bell above my door chimed and heavy, somber boots clipped a steady beat on the floorboards. Someone slowly but surely was navigating my maze of books, and he or she was not a customer, unless I'd lost my wits entirely somewhere between Atlantis and the land of the dead. I didn't bother to lift my head from the unedited pages of my novel on the counter.

Honestly, I didn't care.

"So this is the afterlife?" asked a deep baritone voice.

"Haven't you heard?" I reached below the counter, fetched another glass. "I'm immortal these days, Your Majesty."

I poured Jon Faraday two fingers' worth of Glenlivet 12. He didn't get the spicy 15. Not after his piss poor performance on the Plains of Perdition and the whole exile under pain of death affair. He took the glass with a nod of thanks.

"Yes. That's a rumor spreading faster than wildfire through Forget. Declan Hale, the Immortal King of Atlantis." Faraday chuckled and took a sip. "Certainly not a part of the plan, to feed your legend, but even the very wise cannot see all ends, hmm."

"You let this happen, Gandalf." With a few sad days to think on it, such a miserable conclusion was the only thing that made sense. "What do you want now?"

"You know what I want, Hale." Faraday stroked the rough stubble coating his chin. "The Renegades destroyed, Forget united, and your head on a pike paraded through the streets of Ascension City, amidst the sounds of imperial trumpet calls and wild, mindless ovation."

"Well…" I had to choose my words carefully. "Click your heels three times, Dorothy, and wish real hard."

"I suppose I owe you thanks, in a way. If not for you and your penchant for sticking your nose in where it doesn't belong, Renegade may well have seized the Infernal Clock and used it to destroy us all."

"You let me escape the Fae Palace, didn't you? You let Clare and Ethan think they'd been so clever in their rescue and let me seek Atlantis and undo the Degradation… You played me."

"Let us be honest, Declan. Can we be that, just this once? You wanted to be played." He looked around at my dusty old shop with a sneer of distaste. "Sitting on the bench was insulting for you, wasn't it? After the Tome Wars? You were chewing at the bit to be tagged back in."

"People were hurt. Clare Valentine *suffered*, Jon. She died afraid." Goddamn it, she died without knowing how much I cared. I pressed my thumb and forefinger against my eyelids. "True love never saves the damn day, does it?"

"Her death was a regrettable loss, but look at the outcome—the Degradation undone, Morpheus Renegade, our greatest adversary, dead. His legions are in disarray and treasures lost ten millennia ago are being retrieved from the ruins of Atlantis as we speak. Small regions of Renegade-controlled Forget are rebelling, as word of his death spreads, but that is manageable. This was a win for the home team."

"Emily, his queen, is still out there. She has at least a half-dozen petals from the Infernal Clock as well as the Roseblade."

"And all the reason in the world to want *you* dead." Faraday chuckled. "I fear she will be your problem before mine. But then who can blame her? You've always made better enemies than friends."

"What if I'd failed? What if the Everlasting had barred my path? If Morpheus had killed me before I reached the Infernal Clock and undid the Degradation? If what's left of Tal stopped my heart?" I threw my hands up. "Or a thousand other things that could have gone wrong."

Faraday nodded. "All taken into consideration. If you'd been killed, then that was one less treasonous madman to deal with. Your death would have solidified my powerbase beyond question. It still will, one day—and soon, no doubt. I don't believe your immortality for a moment."

"I'm alive. I *was* dead. That should give you pause."

A cheap romance novel caught his eye, and Faraday pocketed the paperback. "However, you didn't die, did you? Well, not until it didn't matter anymore. But even that didn't keep you down for long. No, you saved the day. And now I'm the king that recovered Atlantis for the people, and the king that destroyed Morpheus Renegade. All roads, Declan... fortune and glory."

"Did you come to gloat?"

"Partly." Faraday helped himself to another splash of scotch. "And partly to make sure you understand that this changes nothing. Your exile stands. Return to Forget and a cell on Starhold will be the least of your concerns."

So, I'd returned to the start of all this, in a way. I let a carefree grin spread across my face. "I'm going to burn your kingdom to the ground and piss on the ashes."

King Faraday finished his drink and shrugged. "Perhaps you will. Take care, little brother."

My fists unclenched as Faraday saw himself out. The desire to fight, to unleash the Will within… was damn near overwhelming. A ripple of tension shuddered through my arm and an impossible door swung wide open in my mind, away in the ether and the Void beyond.

I looked down. The words on the page were glowing.

~~*~*

*The End of
Book One*

Loved Distant Star?

Declan Hale will return in 2013!

Broken Quill

The Reminiscent Exile: Book Two

JOE DUCIE

Cedar Sky Publishing

Bonus Story!

The Forgetful Library

A Tale of the Knights Infernal

I

There are three types of books in the Forgetful Library.

Well, no, that's not right.

There is every type of book in the Forgetful Library.

But that's not right either. Although not entirely wrong.

I'm not explaining this very well. Broken quill! You think I'd have a way with words. I'm the chief librarian of the largest collection of books in all creation and I can neither explain nor define the tomes under my protection. Let me see…

There is a library. Yes, good. Start small, Aloysius, as my father used to say. Keep it simple, stupid. *Rome wasn't built in a day, Al.* Well, it may have been, for all I know—I wasn't there—but the old bastard's words fit just the same.

The library. Or, the Library. I've always thought of it as Library with a capital 'L'. The endless stacks and infinite catalogues carry an air of sentience, after all. An enormous, slumbering awareness as vast as the stars or the space between stars. An intelligence found in the scent of wood shavings, of spilled vanilla and the aroma of freshly cut grass. Of good, old leather and dusty pages.

That starts to paint a pretty picture, does it not? This is a special library. A unique library. Forged to house the books of the abstract. The books of the never-were, the could-have-been, the lonely-and-lost. That's a fanciful yet fine way of putting it, actually.

The books in the Library are infinite and they are of three distinct kinds. A solid enough definition.

Kind the First: The Forgetful Library contains every book *never* written.

Kind the Second: The Forgetful Library contains every book that ever existed and was *lost*.

Kind the Third: The Forgetful Library contains every book found *within* books.

The first two kinds are rather straightforward and speak for themselves. Kind the Third is a bit more wistful, a bit more... intangible. Think of books inside other books. The unpublished cases of Sherlock Holmes mentioned by John Watson on occasion in the actual stories. *The Red Book of Westmarch*, purportedly the source material used by Professor Tolkien for his fantastical tales. Or Lovecraft's mad poet, Abdul Alhazred, and his blasphemous tome of eldritch lore—*The Necronomicon*. All such stories can be found on the polished jarrah shelves of the Forgetful Library. The last is kept in a dungeon of its own, buried deep beneath the earth. It has a habit of attracting... unpleasantness.

Which I suppose is the reason I'm writing all of this down. Recent unpleasantness. The reason I'm writing a story that will never find its way into my Library, for I intend the whole wide world, and every realm of Forget, to know the truth of this matter—to know the truth of my grandson, Declan, and his mistreatment at the hands of the 'lauded' and 'incorruptible' Knights Infernal.

I have never been one for the fight. Aloysius Hale, a tall, bespectacled gentleman with a penchant for bowties and old pocket watches could never be mistaken for a man of action, for a hero.

But I have lived with heroes.

I have walked in their shadow (or lack thereof, as the case of young Declan may be) and watched them fight their wars against men and less than men. Creatures of the Void—monstrosities that would eat the essence of my Library and feast well on the *possibility* of all the Thrice-Kindly works.

The Forgetful Library has existed since the first written word and is much a part of the Story Thread as the books of actual reality, of the books available at your local corner bookshop or, more so these days, *online* in electronic format. I don't resist the change to e-books, as they're known on True Earth (and many other Earths, come to think of it), and the Library has adapted to all the e-books not written, that have never seen a printed page. There is an annex to the left of Persistent Memory which houses all the encyclopaedias of things that never existed fit to burst with e-books. Still, there is something to be said for the weight and heft of a book. Something… simple, stupid. But where was I? Ah, heroes—men and women of the Will.

Like Declan.

He does not deserve the scorn being placed upon his head. King Faraday sits on a stolen throne spinning lies about my grandson and his deeds. Declan fought the Renegades and the Voidlings through two campaigns and carried the mantle of the Knights Infernal with an integrity unmatched. I'm certain—*certain*—he had good reason for doing what he did, for unleashing the Degradation and sealing away the Lost City. For sacrificing Tal Levy, his love, and selling his shadow to Lord Oblivion. I would ask him those reasons, if I could, but his forced exile prohibits such contact. Yet I suppose that is not the tale I set out to write here today.

There are so many myths and legends wrapped around the boy that I imagine the truth is blurred more by the absurd tales than King Faraday's campaign of misinformation (and I write those words knowing full well I forfeit my position in the Library, if not my head). To support Declan now is to court treason. Well, so be it. Here, at least, you will find one small truth. One true story.

Here is a tale of the Forgetful Library and the night Declan Hale bested the devil.

~~*~*

II

Aloysius stood alone in the vast, cathedral-like central dome of the Library with his hands clasped behind his back. Beams of dull orange light cut the marble floors into long squares. He waited patiently, his neatly pressed suit and knotted bowtie belying the panic he felt.

He was alone in the Library, save for the hidden unpleasantness. The entire staff and custodial service had been dismissed for the evening, given what had happened to young Barnaul in the catalogues of Elusive Thought. Aloysius was confident the unpleasantness had been contained to that area of the Library, specifically within the subsections of Bountiful Doubt, but who knew with these things? Declan would, which was why he had been summoned.

Before sunset, the winged messenger had promised. He supposed he had Fenton Creed to thank for that particular piece of magicked mechanical fascination. That wasn't a fair thought, really. A messenger bird that could seek out his grandson across entire worlds, wherever he was on Earth or in Forget, in less than an hour deserved some admiration. It just grated that the overpowered sycophant had a hand in its construction. Aloysius did not care for how Jon Faraday had wrapped Fenton and a dozen other strong-Willed men like him around his little finger. It stank of unbalance.

The Dragon Throne has sat unclaimed for too long.

Ever since King Morrow's command ship flew into the Void. An unbalance, yes, and now... insurrection was on the horizon. The signs were clear.

As the last of the sun's rays scattered indigo light across the crystal walls, the enormous entrance hall doors swung open on silent hinges to admit Declan.

He strode into the Library's lobby grim faced and tall. His dark hair hung lank against his forehead. There was a nasty cut across his cheek and he looked as if sleep was a distant memory of happier times. Declan was not alone. He grasped the hand of a young woman, wearing a white summer blouse stained with what could only be blood. Despite that, she smiled as they drew level with Aloysius.

"Hey, old man," Declan said. "You couldn't have called at a worse time."

"Oh hush," the woman said. Her voice was soft and light, tinged with an exotic accent that made Aloysius think of desert sands and old, wearied ruins. "He was pleased to hear from you, Mr. Hale."

"I don't believe I've had the pleasure..."

"This is Tal." Declan squeezed her hand and allowed his shoulders to slump, to relax, for just a moment. "Tal Levy."

"Aloysius Hale." They shook hands. Tal's knuckles were torn and bloody. "Where have you two been?"

"The *Reach*. We... we forced the Knights and the Renegades into a final confrontation. It may have even caused your problems here, Grandfather."

"Oh?"

Declan released a long, slow breath. "Yes. For better or worse, the Tome Wars end tonight. But first we deal with the Voidling. Your message said it had already killed? A scribe?"

"It left very little of the man, I'm sorry to say."

"Sounds like a scout. One of the higher order. It was clever. Most of them are just grunts, mindless and cruel, but not this one. If not for the Library's inherent security, it would likely have gone unnoticed."

"You know its type then, lad?"

Declan shrugged. There was a fire in his eyes that warred with his beaten, bloodied fatigue. "Perhaps. Given the damage caused to the *Reach*, this would be the most opportune location for it to try and come through. Reality is bleeding, after all. Lead the way and we'll see."

"Are you sure you're up for this, Declan?" Tal asked. "You can barely stand."

Aloysius dabbed at the blood on his grandson's cheek with a chequered handkerchief. "I share this young lady's concerns."

Declan smiled and limped off into the Library proper. Each of his steps left a bloody track on the pristine marble floors.

~~*~*

III

"I'm going in alone, songbird."

"Like fun you are." Tal grasped Declan's forearm.

"The more minds it can touch the stronger it becomes. I can beat it one on one. Got my brain all sauced up. You know that. But not if it has a hook in your head."

A small blush rose high in Tal's olive cheeks. "Why?"

He laughed. "You going to make me say it again, huh?"

Tal dug her nails into his skin.

"Ow, alright." He sighed. "I love you. I am in love with you. I want to kiss you and touch you and dance with you. Tal Levy, you're my girl and right now, to this creature, that's a weakness I can't afford. It will use you against me and we'll both die."

Satisfied, Tal released Declan's arm and smiled. "Okay."

Declan blinked, cast a quick look at his grandfather, and shrugged. "Oh its that easy, is it? You get what you want and I get to face a horrific nightmare that eats people and devours their souls."

Aloysius removed a long, silver key from a chain around his neck and handed it to Declan. "This should get you in, lad. We'll be able to see you on the screens from the vestibule here."

Along the far wall was a bank of monitors. In the centre screen was a catalogue of books that had been... *warped*. A dark, swirling vortex of inky blackness rippled through the books. It was a hole in reality, a step into the Void.

"No farewell kiss?"

Tal licked her lips. "You'll get one when you come back in one piece, Hale."

"I like her, Declan," Aloysius said. "I should tell you to be careful, but I honestly have no idea what is happening beyond that door. The catalogues of Bountiful Doubt contain fictitious, often mean spirited book of the never-were. Perhaps knowing that will help you. How will you fight this thing?"

Declan's blue eyes sparkled in the half-light of the electric globes on the lavish walls. True night had fallen outside the Library. "You have to outsmart the bastards, Grandfather."

"And how will—?"

"Riddles," Tal said. "We were always taught to strike at the Void with riddles."

Aloysius blinked. "Why is a raven like a writing desk?"

Declan stepped across the corridor and unlocked the heavy doors. "Something like that." He opened the entrance a crack and peeked into the catalogue. Then, without another word, slipped into the darkness and closed the door gently behind him.

It was cold in the immense rooms of Bountiful Doubt. Large wooden bookshelves lined the walls, fit to burst with leather bound tomes. The heady scent of grass shavings and old vanilla was pungent and overpowering. Declan knew Tal was only a handful of gorgeous steps away, back through the door, but it felt more like miles. He pulled his jacket close about himself and tread lightly across the polished floor.

He was not alone, of that he could be certain. The small wound in his side throbbed, dripping down his jeans and into his boot. It was foolish to have come here straight from what had happened at the *Reach*, but he was a Knight—and this was his duty.

The creature was waiting for him in the heart of the open room.

It stood wreathed in darkness, alongside the warped portal in the stacks he had seen on the monitors out in the foyer. Reading desks with comfy velvet-backed chairs held the no man's land between Declan and the Voidling. A distance of only about ten feet.

The creature gave no sign that it knew he was there. That it could see him or anything at all.

Declan swung one of the ornate wooden chairs around and sat down with his arms crossed over the back. He stared at the tall, thin monster cloaked in midnight blue and grinned. A band of cool sweat broke out across his forehead.

A minute slipped by.

Another.

During the third minute, blood began to drip from Declan's nose. Then from his eyes.

The fourth minute was unremarkable.

At five minutes, the creature flinched and made a sound below hearing. Like a chime in the back of the mind. It screamed.

Only then did Declan speak.

"You're a strong one," he said. "And you have more form than most of your brethren. Leave now or be destroyed."

Skeletal hands clenched around the folds of its robe. The vortex spinning inside the warped stacks of books shimmered, as if a pebble had been cast on still waters. Beyond lay the Void, an expanse of infinite nothing that would devour everything if this monster were left unchecked.

"Shadowless, you will stand aside."

"I think not." *Shadowless?* He had no idea what that meant. Declan estimated the spinning vortex was expanding a few inches every minute. It would be tied to the creature, tethered to reality.

"What is this place?"

"The abstract distinct, my friend. Raw magic refined into science. Chaos into order. The Forgetful Library, a work of staggering genius. It has grown vast and cruel, like a razor blade slicing through worlds and into your Void. This is why you were drawn here."

The creature made a sound halfway between a laugh and a growl. *"We choose here to leave the Void."*

"No. No, you do not."

Declan braced himself against the chair as a wave of force slammed into his mind. A blizzard of rampant, dark energy—of the space outside of the universe—of the nothing, of the Void. It tickled and he laughed.

"You'll have to do better than that!" He cracked his knuckles. "Say my name and I disappear. What am I?"

The creature recoiled as if stung. *"Silence. The more you take, the more you leave behind…"*

"Footsteps. Tall in the morning, short at noon, gone in the evening yet due back soon—"

"A shadow," the Voidling rasped, and laughed. *"How apt. Voiceless it cries, wingless flutters, toothless bites, mouthless mutters. What is it?"*

"The wind. At dusk the silent sentinels arrive without being summoned. At dawn they flee without being stolen. What are they?"

The creature hissed and spluttered. It writhed on the spot, tethered to both realms of reality and nothing. Its time ran out. A long, hideous slash split its robes and the pallid flesh beneath. Declan relaxed and licked the blood from his lips. It didn't know the answer. Accords as old as the universe declared him victor of the contest.

"I bind you to my Will," he said, as if discussing the weather over a glass of something red. "Through accorded contest you are bested."

"*The answer, Shadowless! I will have the answer!*" Its lips cracked and came apart, digging deep scars, a repugnant grin, up into its cheeks.

"The stars. The distant stars arrive at dusk and flee at dawn. You know them not in your damned realm, and you are bound for it. Now, we have observed the niceties—we've matched wits, minds, and wisdom—you will leave this place and return to the Void. I have business this evening far more important than you."

"*I will return for you... Shadowless.*"

"It will be some time before your kind find such a convenient hole in the world again, I think. Now. *Be gone.*"

The Voidling crumpled like a Coke can hit by a car. It folded back into the vortex between the shelves and mangled tomes of the Thrice-Kindly works. A great scream, the collective voices of a million cheated monstrosities from beyond time and space, slammed against Declan's fortified mind and glanced off as the path to Hell snapped shut.

The scream rattled his wits. Declan leaned over and vomited up the last thing he'd eaten—two fingers worth of scotch and a jam donut. A kingly breakfast, given the day he'd had and the night to come.

All in all, a job well done. *S'pose I just saved a fair old chunk of Forget.*

He stood up, swayed on the spot for a moment, and then nodded. Declan strolled back through the stacks at ease, his face a mask of dried blood. He unlocked the doors of Bountiful Doubt and exited the catalogue. Tal and Aloysius were waiting just beyond the vestibule.

Tal was as white as snow. "You fought it and won," she said, amazed. "How?"

"Charm, good looks and a winning attitude, my dear. You caught most of the exchange, Grandfather?"

Aloysius shook his head. "There was too much distance, son. It looked like it had you for a moment there."

Declan grinned. "Not even close. Let me tell you the story."

~~*~*

IV

And as he told it to me, I tell it to you now.

Declan Hale outwitted the vanguard of a Voidling army on the eve of his Degradation. Tired and alone, he faced the horror beyond the edge of creation and laughed. King Faraday of the Knights Infernal, King Morpheus Renegade and his Immortal Queen call him a fiend—a heathen pretender to the throne. Yet those of us who knew him know the truth. He never fought for the throne, because his heart was broken. He *allowed* himself to be exiled.

I have lived with heroes.

This Library on the very edge of Forget, overseen by an old man, has caught the blood of the genuine king.

The Fae Palace at the heart of Ascension City hosts false dominion over Forget. My grandson ended the war, saved countless worlds and lost his love and his shadow in the bargain. He is owed our allegiance and our throne... and if this is to be my treason, then so be it:

Long live Declan Hale, Shadowless Arbiter, the High Lord and True King of the Forgetful Realms.

~~*~*

ABOUT THE AUTHOR

Joe Ducie (1987-) is a writer from Perth, Western Australia. By day, he charges a toll to cross a bridge he doesn't own. Yet by night, in a haze of scotch-fuelled insanity, he works tirelessly on an array of stories both short and long. Joe possesses a fierce love of a smooth finish. Under no circumstances should you ask him just what that means.

Joe was born in Barrow-in-Furness, Cumbria in November 1987, and currently resides in Perth, Western Australia. He is primarily an author of urban fantasy and science fiction aimed at young adults. His current stories include *Distant Star, Upon Crystal Shores, Red vs. Blue*, and *The Forgetful Library*.

Joe attended Edith Cowan University and graduated in 2010 with a Degree of Counterterrorism, Security and Intelligence. He went back, the idiot, and completed post-graduate studies in Security Science in 2011.

When not talking about himself in the third person, Joe enjoys devouring books at an absurdly disgusting rate and sampling fine scotch.

Website: joeducie.net
Twitter: @joeducie
Facebook: /jducie

Made in the USA
Middletown, DE
08 May 2020

93444515R00135